όσ[illegible]ολοι
ρυθμό,
ίας.Στο
αχτερό-

New Moon: Day One

THANASSIS VALTINOS

New Moon: Day One

Translated by Jane Assimakopoulos and Stavros Deligiorgis

Laertes

Chapel Hill, North Carolina

Cover and book design by Maxine Mills

Printed in the United States of America

First Edition

New Moon: Day One was first published as Νέα Σελήνη. Ημέρα πρώτη by Hestia Publishers, copyright © 2022 by Thanassis Valtinos.

PUBLISHER CATALOGING-IN-PUBLICATION DATA

Names: Valtinos, Thanasēs - author. | Assimakopoulos, Jane - translator. | Deligiorgis, Stavros, 1933 - translator, author of introduction.

Title: Thanassis Valtinos : New Moon: Day One / translated by Jane Assimakopoulos and Stavros Deligiorgis.

Description: Chapel Hill, North Carolina : Laertes Press, 2024.

Other titles: Prose works. English.

Identifiers: LCCN 2023943304 | ISBN 9781942281351 (softcover : alk. paper)

Classification: LCC PA5633.A4 N4313 2024 | DDC 889.34 — V248

Laertes

www.laertesbooks.org

CONTENTS

ιόφορ

INTRODUCTION

The Making of a Writer: the Making of an Age

Thanassis Valtinos's most recent novel, *New Moon: Day One* has reconfirmed, as did all his previous books, his reputation as a master portraitist of the 20th century, skillfully delineating the times and events before and after the painful midpoint of the Greek nineteen-forties. As a writer also of minimalist exposition and subtle nuance Valtinos has tapped once again into his readers' most guarded contradictions vis-à-vis their lives in times of transition, annihilation, and transformation. Judging by the reissue of so many of his past masterpieces, Valtinos's readers must still be visiting his narratives at a steady rate for no other reason than their love of his memorable cadences and the worldviews underlying them.

By way of background, Valtinos's Greece between 1897 and 1923, and well prior to his birth in 1932, was a gravely traumatized country with a gutted economy and an ever more polarized society. Richly as the creative domain fared during both the best and the worst of times, surprisingly, Greece, as a less than one-hundred-year-old state, was strangely divided on the question of a foundational, unified, and unifying linguistic voice. Bloody clashes between police and demonstrators had already taken place between 1901 and 1903 in Athens over such issues as the translation of New Testament books from their original Koine Greek into Modern Greek, and of Aeschylus's *Oresteia* from its 5th century BCE Attic Greek into its 20th century direct descendant as Modern Greek.

The setting for the main action of Valtinos's new book is an unspecified rural capital in the Peloponnese during the penultimate stages of the Greek government 1948 operations to uproot communist insurgency from the countryside. One might say that the 1943 to 1948 ideologically motivated civil war was one more sign of the same disunity that prevailed earlier in Greece's linguistic arena, only writ large. The author, like his protagonists in *New Moon: Day One,* was a middle school student at the time of these internecine conflicts and had firsthand knowledge of what it was like to see his native village's 118 houses burned to the ground and hundreds of his fellow villagers dragged in moving camps of barefoot hostages who would eventually be dumped, by way of disposal, into dry pits to die.

But as Greece was taking its first tottering steps after the Second World War, and just as the arts were picking up where they had left off before the war, there were tens of thousands of leftists still in island concentration camps and homes of detention. The young Valtinos had seen enough cruelty on both sides of the ideological rift to be able to go on living and working as if nothing had happened and without taking sides. He has never minced his words about the roots of his writing or about writing from a moderate Greek's perspective.

Seasoned idealists were at work during those grim times, however, whose collective output might be seen as an effort to realign their hundred-year-old country both with its intellectual past and its creative present in a rapidly modernizing Europe. "The Generation of the '30s," as they were called, was made up of about 20 dedicated artists and writers who would soon model a broader outlook on the question of poetry, primarily, as the constitutive bond of the Greek identity. Two distinguished men of letters would soon stand out from this group to international recognition, Giorgos Seferis (Nobel Prize, 1963) and Odysseus Elytis (Nobel Prize, 1979), not merely for their important contributions as authors to world literature but also as active bridge-makers, via the unsung craft of translation. Seferis's vision included making the major Anglo-American poets, like Ezra Pound and T. S. Eliot, better known in Greek. Elytis steadily transferred scores of his French contemporary surrealists into Greece's critical purview.

Even the young Valtinos of the mid-nineteen-forties did not escape the pervasive ethnocentrism of the Generation of the '30s. He reveals, in the course of an interview, that Cosmas Politis's 1936 novel *Eroica,* rated among the 100 best Greek books ever written, had so enthralled him as an adolescent he refused to reread it ever since.[1] The vivid memory of that experience is encapsulated in the cast of *New Moon*'s student characters — their literature instructor bears the same last name as in Politis's *Eroica!* — but also in Valtinos's deliberate portrayal of their outlook, in stark contrast to Politis's youths, as markedly anti-heroic. Politis, by the end of his life, and true to the Generation of the '30s re-empowering agenda, had eighteen books of fiction to his name and no fewer than fifty-two books of translations from four languages.

Valtinos's post-secondary education in Athens in the early 1950s coincided with the unqualified best of the Generation of the '30s but also with an increased awareness of the wealth that the Greek oral tradition could bring to Greek modernism. When asked about his "origins" as a writer, Valtinos misses no opportunity to extoll his admiration for the anonymous folk songs he had both read and grew up with in his native Arcadia. The songs form a body of verse noted for its manly ethos, as well as its amatory, funereal, and tragic subjects. A printed version, assembled by the inspired folklorist Nikolaos Politis, became available in 1914 in a standard selection for every Greek to consult. These folksongs, with their particular diction and drama, their breathtaking brevity, and their fragmentariness, are, according to Valtinos, the heart and soul of his work. He also adds an admiring coda to the effect that the

1. Transcriptions of statements by Thanassis Valtinos in Greek can be sourced to Kostis Danopoulos, ed., *Opos o Erotas* ([Writing is] Like Love), *Interviews 1972–2018*, Estia Publ., 2020; 50 recorded discussions covering vast areas of criticism, autobiography, historical literary forms, the process of writing, the structure of particular stories, the classical tradition, his novels and plays. Danopoulos treats these interpersonal exchanges as anything but ephemera. They are an integral part of Valtinos's creative work, a sizable number of which have been reprinted from cohesive cycles of meditative, prose-poem-like essays. Re: Valtinos's specific refusal to reread Politis's *Eroica* in order not to dispel the impression it had made on him when he first read it, this is mentioned in Kostis Danopoulos's article "On Thanassis Valtinos's *New Moon [: Day One],"* Athens periodical *O Anagnostis*, April 30, 2022, pp. 1–24, esp. 15, footnote 40, dating it to an earlier publication in *Krasi kai nymphes* (*Wine and Nymphs: Short Texts on Everything [Knowable]*), Estia Publ., 2009, pp. 140–141.

songs' enduring presence in his native culture is achieved through a spare, 1500-word vocabulary grand total.[2]

The Greek folk songs, however, which to all appearances are so narrowly local, also host themes and attitudes, according to Politis's research, that are traceable to universal archetypes harkening back to the early Proto-Indo-European civilization! Could it be then that this innate universality is the key to the haunting appeal Valtinos's oeuvre holds for so many diverse audiences the world over and in all the languages into which he has been and continues to be translated?

As far as Valtinos's formation of a storytelling idiom is concerned, he does acknowledge the role American cinema played when it had reached the city of his youth around 1948. Hollywood's seductive scenes were continually projected in the far recesses of Arcadia prefecture's provincial capital, even as deadly battles were being fought all around it. Cinema to the young meant escaping from the repression of all forms of sensuality that took place in their homes, and forgetting themselves in the endless loop of westerns, musicals, Pacific Ocean landscapes, murder mysteries, and space cartoons. The technology was brilliant and contagious. Dailies would announce that in a given year Greece had hit a lamentable high of eight divorces while adjacent columns reported American, French, and Italian stars' stormy liaisons, which became Greek household gossip in no time at all.

The day soon came, however, when Valtinos began attending university, taking courses in law and political science in Athens. The new environment came with more "real" cinema by the likes of Orson Wells, Frank Capra, Ingmar Bergman, René Clair, Akira Kurosawa, and Roberto Rossellini, to name but a few. Athens had real theater too that staged Ibsen, Shakespeare, and live Aristophanes. There were schools too where one could learn the crafts of the visual arts like script writing and directing and where contemporaries of

2. Article in Greek, Kostis Danopoulos, "Researching the Sources of the Novel *The Alonnisos Journal* by Thanassis Valtinos," in *Political Changeover 1974–1981: Literature and Cultural History*, eds., Giannis Dimitrakakis, Anastasia Natsina, Publications of the University of Crete, School of Philosophy, Rethymno, 2021, pp. 167–182. On Valtinos's working with and teaching at Karolos Koun's Art Theater School, p. 173.

Valtinos could be met and conversed with on equal terms — something he had the opportunity to do when he briefly attended one such school.

Two and a half decades following the first success in 1958 of a prizewinning short story, and through the three successive book-length stunners *The Descent of the Nine* (1963), *The Book of Andreas Kordopatis* (1964), and *Three One-Act Greek Plays* (1976), Valtinos presented a palette of Greece itself in which hundreds of thousands of immigrant-emigrant refugees, tens of thousands of political exiles, and fast-aging, lonely urbanites could see themselves reflected with unprecedented clarity and compassion. The range as well as the originality of his publications soon earned Valtinos the position of teaching Greek literature at Karolos Koun's prestigious Theater actors' school between 1978 and 1982.[3] Teaching at the very hub of Koun's projects, in turn, was to lead to the performance in Valtinos's translation of Aeschylus's *Persians* under Koun's direction at the Epidaurus international festival in 1979. The play is of the identical cloth as that of Valtinos's earlier stories of elegiac loss in his *Descent of the Nine* and *Addiction to Nicotine.* Translating Aeschylus's *Persians* — a play suffused by a spirit of commiseration for the defeated — is also key for the dark prose of Valtinos on the recent Greek Civil War: It stands apart from the previous fifty-year-old philological canon of translations in general and it resonates with the notoriously antiheroic poet Archilochus who had lived even before Aeschylus. The Epidaurus venue, it should be said in passing, in those days as in ours, meant the introduction of the author to audiences as large as 17,000 seats per single show.

When Valtinos's short story "Addiction to Nicotine," depicting the 1948 military anti-insurgency operations in the Peloponnese, came out in 1979, Valtinos went on record a few years later saying that he "always wanted to fulfill a repressed urge to make a movie out of that story" under the relatively flat title "First Night After the New Moon."[3] That was the beginning of the long gestation that lasted well into the twenty-twenties of the novel we now know as *New Moon: Day One.*

3. Article in Greek, Kostis Danopoulos, "Thanassis Valtinos' *New Moon [: Day One],"* Athens periodical *O Anagnostis*, April 30, 2022, esp. p. 3, n. 12.

A New Novel; a New Miracle

The title of the book alone, *New Moon: Day One*, prefigures a sublunar "interpretive framework," as Erving Goffman[4] would have said, for its readers as well as its characters. Scenes like a love-struck young man's life-threatening bicycle acrobatics, or provincial youths ogling traveling vaudeville posters, appear to be conducted in plain daylight, yet they touch on barely veiled urges of the twin forces of Eros and Thanatos in Valtinos's hands. Valtinos probes the ethology of abjection and desire that couldn't be further removed from the visible solar spectrum. A succession of mostly brief scenes encourages the reader to join the invisible, and close to inaudible, narrator in suspending judgment until the final segments of the novel, which may or may not affect the reader's ultimate overview. Could the ending stand as a whole for the times of the action? Or, more precisely, could it stand for the whole composite, not just the genteel façades of post-WWII times in Greek small towns?

Valtinos's latest work, like all his previous novels, appears to have broken ranks with the prevalent esthetics of their predecessors. His fiction seems to dialogue, critically and silently, with both the old and the new arts that circumvent didacticism, linearity, and resolution. Emphasis on pauses, recurrent dissonances, and mixed textures of third person points of view, and "sign" tagged first person snatches that could have been recorded by a bystander all have the markings of a Karl-Heinz Stockhousen electronic composition[5] and of the cutting room of cinema verité editing. The building blocks of *New Moon* could be compared to the rolling out of an Igor Stravinsky string of syncopated tempi that, at some unspecified moment, permit the measures of a Russian

4. Canadian-born American sociologist (1922–1982). Erving Goffman's titles are more than plain: *Frame Analysis: An Essay on the Organization of Experience*, Harper and Row, 1974; and *Forms of Talk,* University of Pennsylvania Press, 1981.

5. Danopoulos reconstructs the precise personal circumstances that led Valtinos to explore and apply electronic music's nonlinear "concrete" poetics to his novel *Alonnisos Journal*. Valtinos's intermediary was Dimitris Iatropoulos, who had studied these radical arts in Austria and Germany. See op. cit. (note 2) above, pp. 175–6.

folk song to break through, though these may still not hold any promise of resolution to the whole.

From the translation frenzy of his elders and from his own experience as translator for the theater, Valtinos gleaned the trained ear for the twofold dynamic of any single classic play: The use of the Ionic dialect for verse soliloquies and dialog; and the Doric dialect for the purposes of the collective, meditative song and dance poetry of the chorus. *New Moon: Day One* uses tonal shifts between the detached reportage of interpersonal communication and the descriptive, widescreen segments where talk is superfluous. Long before the ending of *New Moon* the reader has been trained to listen, like a modernist, for clashing juxtapositions, grating disparities, and suggestive, mystical undertones beyond words.

Twentieth Century Fauna

The urban and rural Greeces that emerge from the illuminating premises of Valtinos's *New Moon* modulate on older cultural strata as they do in Politis's *Eroica,* but with fewer certainties to them. Apropos of the living classical past in our midst, as T. S. Eliot would have put it, there is also William Faulkner's explanation of the titling of his major 1932 novel, *Light in August*:

> In August in Mississippi there's a few days somewhere about the middle of the month when suddenly there's a foretaste of fall, it's cool, there's a lambency, a soft, a luminous quality to the light, as though it came not from just today but from back in the old classic times. It might have fauns and satyrs and the gods and — from Greece, from Olympus in it somewhere. It lasts just for a day or two, then it's gone . . . the title reminded me of that time, of a luminosity older than our Christian civilization.[6]

6. Hugh Ruppersburg, *Reading Faulkner: Light in August*, Univ. Press of Mississippi, 1994, p. 5. Ever since Stéphane Mallarmé's 1876 poem and eventual Debussy-Nijinsky choreography *L'Après-midi d'un faune* (The Afternoon of a Faun), "fauns and satyrs" are shorthand for classically inspired thematics.

By sheer coincidence, there is a shopkeeper, described as a "middle-aged satyr," in Valtinos's *New Moon,* who plays a joke on the novel's young protagonists with a gag camera.

Regarding his own mining of the whole of the European past, Valtinos fortuitously yet explicitly echoes Faulkner's way of thinking: "The things I write have been written about since time immemorial. I just reach back and mine them."[7] His high school youths, certainly by instinct, conflate Freud's hypothesis of risk and despair in their cartoon-like sketch of their French teacher's pubic area under the label of the "triangle of death." When, as later related by one of these youths to another, she herself replaces the caption with the words "triangle of life," this does not in the least diminish the force of the two spectacular incidents that take place in the town square on that day: the making of the rounds in a horse-drawn buggy by the local brothel's reigning queen in all her finery for everyone to admire; and the dark counterpart of an army truckload of dead men and women rebels dumped there for all to see and shudder at.

Fiction, like all of the other arts, luxuriates in what is not expressed. Unresolvable ambiguities and constant recontextualizations are the order of the day. Shifts between indoor and outdoor settings in this novel, for instance, airbrush the differences between the private and the communal spaces. Readers and characters alike internalize complex experiences with the rapidity of a glance. Events are perceived as large-scale puzzles which, once solved, only confirm the readers' initial deductions from silence. Elision by implication, conciseness, and compression may be better terms to describe the musicality of Valtinos's style and the rhythms of his exposition. His minimalism couldn't be closer to Keats's "sweeter music" that is not heard, from his "Ode on a Grecian Urn," than that which is. Oblique devices like irony, opprobrium, or innuendo as elements of the colloquial poetics of everyday speech explode on almost every page of *New Moon.*

7. Grigoris Bekos, "Interview," in Greek, Athens daily *To Vima*, May 19, 2022.

Page one, Section 1, starts out with the conventional *descriptio temporis* of the year, a fast dip into a foreign language drill with a young, left-handed female teacher in a boys' school. A drawing is made of her from behind on a piece of paper with a caption warning of the mortal danger between her legs. The paper soon transforms into a dart which lands in the aisle between the rows of desks under the teacher's stern gaze. The dual mood of youthful levity on one hand and the young teacher's professional look on the other will be offset, in reverse, in Section 2 by the flamboyant appearance of the town brothel's Madame, provoking the male population in the central square, gawking at her as she parades before them.

As the come-one, come-all show closes, everyone snaps back to the day-to-day affairs in the commercial town hub. The bus depot is filling up with passengers. A pharmacy has just dispensed medication for a distant patient. Outdoor noise — the low hum of business-as-usual — is broken by the grinding rumble of army personnel carriers that are part of the ongoing Civil War "special ops" in progress. Indoor quiet will also be broken in a student's rented room behind the storefronts, where an adolescent places a chair on top of a table so he and a classmate can better view a neighboring woman's semi-nudity — reconnoitering that soon ends in a deafening crash. It is not just the reader, but the entire town that is now back to Section 1 and the abyss between the surface hustle and the hidden bustle of craving for the mature female to take notice.

The Novel in Blank on White

The design of the book, the size of its chapters strikingly unequal, some of them barely one short paragraph long, are nothing less than the impulses that energize the exposition into brisk readability. The heartbeat of Valtinos's prose and its fast pace are a result of the combination of suggestive data in each paragraph and their framing within the generous neutral spaces surrounding them.

Freestanding short lines, as in Section 10, which concludes the long Day 1 with a funeral ceremony, or Section 16 which, for all the world, reads like an exquisite translation of Ezra Pound's 1913 imagist verses "In a Station of the

Metro," act as punctuation pieces. Taken in isolation they could stand for "airs" and meditative pauses between the otherwise crowded and busy sections of the book. *New Moon's* Section 16 turn-of-the-century *Japonisme,* in its elliptical syntax, its veiled and subdued ambience afloat in the printer's ink-free page, is a prose poem that functions, like its look-alikes, as the golden thread of a choral commentary on the main narrative's overview. Basic physical and communal existence in Section 18 (waking up from a wet dream on a rainy day), Section 28 (a freeze frame at the flagpole), and Section 46 (morning chocolate milk snack during recess), all culminate in the sardonic Section 47 describing the preening ritual of the pompous and penurious "national" poet visiting the school on the recommendation of a local army commander.

The user's manual, however, in Section 55, regarding brothel protocols — the novel ends ambiguously as to whether or not they were followed by the boys, and also as to whether or not the boys themselves follow in the footsteps of the national poet — is typical of every other cluster of images or ideas in a holding pattern that hovers not on the page but on the reader's construing of absent settings. And this is precisely where the art of this novel resides. The vagueness of the literature teacher's profile is more than counterbalanced by his students' engaging him on the subject of faith. The French teacher's figure drawn on a paper plane is nothing by comparison to the actual fantasy of a physical intrusion into her residence. The sensation of the classroom desk seats emanating the warmth of girls' bodies disperses into thin air before the brusque slap of a pair of panties landing on the principal's face. The venal visiting poet's pose is pulverized by its juxtaposition with the mention of writers like Stendhal and Odysseus Elytis. Madame Africana's instructing her prostitutes to rise to the roles of professional mourners in the local cathedral is a genuine performer's metamorphosis in response to a heavy, ritual requirement for the pampering of the dead.

Being and Becoming

New Moon: Day One is not a case study; it is not a document or the précis of a memoir; it is not the chronicle of a bygone era, the story board with Post-it size directions for a social studies project. It is definitely not a *Bildungsroman* (in which no one's character is informed in any particular way) nor an *Erziehungsroman* (in which no specific values lead to a character's integration in a significant cultural pattern). Nor is it a *Tom-Sawyer*-cum-*Huckleberry-Finn* adventures-and-merry-pranks yarn (with signs or experiences of bonding between characters). *New Moon* is not a rite-of-passage saga (there are no preliminary or postliminary strictly traditional constraints for any of the characters in the novel), or a coming of age reverie (aside from the attending puerilities of clandestine smoking and outright trespassing in peoples' back yards). War machines may be thundering not too far from the edge of one's neighborhood, but there is enough electricity to run Hollywood movies. Stationery stores still carry ink sacs for Parker pens; hotels still host military brass romantic assignations, and books can still be read and borrowed from the local library. But search as one may, apart from the mention of a remote village, no one in this novel shares a sense of place or belonging, nor any drama of self or class manifestos in times past and present, nor interest in travel, learning, or serving. Nowhere is there a fund of family memories, heirlooms, or exploits. *New Moon: Day One* could easily be the embodiment of Wallace Stevens's desideratum in the 3 epigraphs to his "Notes towards a Supreme Fiction" (1942):

> It must be abstract . . .
> It must change . . .
> It must give pleasure . . .

The novel does not have a design upon the reader. It is no single individual's conception of what it is, including its author who may happen to be its first, but not necessarily its most discerning, reader. It invites and rewards analysis.

Even as it is being unpacked, it imparts bursts of kaleidoscopic intensity. It is a self-sustaining abstraction that can conveniently be labeled art because it supports and integrates the interrelations of its parts in spite of the myriad logical objections that it doesn't.

Speaking of things missing, forlorn, or void of meaning, Valtinos's penultimate Section 54 of *New Moon* opens on a deserted train station office, its tabletop telegraph ticking on and on, aimlessly, with no one in attendance except for two of the novel's protagonists who are wandering across the tracks and who walk gradually away from each other in the mist. Two parallels come to mind: first, the post-apocalyptic frame with neither a sender's nor a receiver's Morse code dots and dashes in Stanley Kramer's 1959 film adaptation of Neville Shute's novel *On the Beach* (1957); and, second, our author's conscious anchoring of his stories' roots in the primal idiom of the earliest surviving dramatist Aeschylus and, unconsciously, drawing on the earliest lyricist and openly antiheroic Archilochus (c. 680–c. 645 BCE). The latter, like Valtinos, was someone with no illusions about sexuality or a soldier's sense of duty to hearth and regiment. Even when Valtinos's peaceable countrymen find themselves caught in the crosshairs of ongoing military operations, the poet's voice will still be heard echoing the ancient song about man's limitations and yearning for survival and beauty.

—*Stavros Deligiorgis*

NEW MOON ● DAY ONE

ά έτοιμα να

ην πραμάτεια

στέρηση. Ακ

ντα. Ο πατέ

ι, βιαστικά

DAY ONE

1.

1948. Winter. A classroom. The French teacher at the blackboard conjugating the verb "*vouloir*." Her voice is accompanied by the sound of the chalk crumbling against the hard surface.

Some of the students are taking notes. Others simply watch. Kosmas, bent over his notebook, is sketching the French teacher with her back to him, her left hand with the chalk raised, her skirt gently tugging upward, partially revealing her thighs. She is left-handed.

Satisfied, he stops, looking over the result from a bit further back. With two strokes of the pencil, he corrects the line of her underarm and draws a vertical arrow directly between her parted legs: To the "Triangle of Death."

The student next to him nudges him. Startled, Kosmas goes to cover his notebook with his hands, then relaxes. It is only someone from the other side of the classroom trying to signal something to him. Kosmas writes something on the side of the paper with the sketch, tears it out, folds it into a paper plane and launches it in his direction. Without stopping what she is saying, the French teacher turns toward the class. Kosmas freezes. With her sentence cut short midway, the teacher watches the paper plane as it lands with one final swoop in the aisle. The protracted silence that follows is broken by chuckling coming from the back row of desks. The teacher looks sternly in that direction and slowly walks toward the aisle.

2.

A sunny winter day. A horse-and-buggy with its hood drawn back moves along the main street of a provincial town. To the right and to the left buildings, old and low, mostly two-story. Some movement on the sidewalks. Hardly any traffic. The coachman with his back turned. Gaunt, old, he wears heavy gloves and a knitted woolen cap pulled down to his ears. Every so often, as though it were a tic, he throws up his hands and snaps the reins in the air to maintain a steady pace. Without slowing down, the buggy turns into the town square. There is more activity here. On the eastern edge of the square beneath the bare lindens, a row of shoeshine stands.

The entrance of the buggy is strongly felt. Many heads turn toward it. Some people strolling idly about stop to watch it as it continues making its way at the same pace around the square. In its quilted back seat a young woman. In flashy dress but with a tasteful color scheme. Stiff and remote, she is completely indifferent to the curiosity and the concealed interest caused by her passing.

At the next corner the buggy turns and leaves the square. The track left behind by her allure now closes.

3.

A narrow commercial street. The shops ready to close. The employees are collecting and putting away the merchandise. Kosmas, out of breath, as though he were late in arriving. He follows his father. They are carrying various packages. The father is about fifty, full of energy. He looks younger. He walks ahead with long, sure steps.

FATHER: I was expecting to eat with you.

KOSMAS: (*apologetically*) They kept us late today. They changed our schedule.

The father stops outside of a pharmacy. He gives Kosmas one of the packages he is carrying to free his hands.

FATHER: Hold this so I can get your grandmother's drops.

He pushes the door and goes inside. The door closes behind him automatically. Posted on the door-pane a round clearly visible sign: "No Military Allowed on the Premises."

Kosmas waits on the sidewalk, peering inside. An old-fashioned pharmacy. Its shelves painted with off-white oil paint, and in its large drawers small oval enameled signs with Latin characters on them.

The cathedral clock strikes two. At that moment the whir of a car is heard. From the end of the street a military jeep appears. Behind it a small truck followed by two larger ones. Next to the driver of the jeep an officer in a helmet and combat uniform. The trucks filled with armed soldiers. The father exits the pharmacy and stops to watch the small convoy pass them by. The soldiers' faces silent and closed beneath the canvas hoods.

The father takes the package he had given him from Kosmas's hands.

FATHER: Let's get going or I'll miss my bus.

At the next corner the convoy turns right. Kosmas and his father follow. They turn at the same corner. The trucks have disappeared from view. The father still walking ahead.

KOSMAS: How is Grandma?

FATHER: She's not well.

KOSMAS: Why didn't you bring her so the doctors could see her?

FATHER: Because she didn't want to come. You know her when she makes up her mind.

They walk along the sidewalk on the left. On the opposite side of the street is a "Distillery and Chandler" shop. Two wooden candles hang from hooks on either side of the door. A man is bent over latching shut the drawn-down metal blinds. Behind them another whir from a vehicle is heard, much louder this time. Two tanks veer toward them furiously. The stooping man gets up and watches them approach. Kosmas and his father have also paused. The roar grows louder, and as the tanks go past them, they see the man across the street gesturing and shouting loudly.

MAN: What's going on? What's happening?

Someone answers him from a window somewhere but it cannot be heard. Kosmas raises his head toward him. A third man interjects.

THIRD MAN: They attacked Monodendri.

Passersby have begun to gather. The father pulls at Kosmas.

FATHER: Let's go, I'll miss the bus.

4.

An empty space between the houses. A vacant lot. Four or five buses that provide transportation to various villages. One of them, already full, is turning to leave. Someone in charge shouts instructions at the driver.

Come on . . . this way . . . come on.

His voice is drowned out by the din of people caught up in the endless commotion. On the roof of another bus, an assistant ready to cover and tie the luggage. He sees Kosmas and his father approaching hurriedly.

ASSISTANT: You're late, Dimitris.

There is a kind of panic in his impatience. Without speaking the father begins tossing him the packages he and Kosmas are holding one by one. Many of the passengers have already boarded the bus. The father, his hands free, takes out some money and gives it to Kosmas.

FATHER: This is for your shoes. Try them on first to make sure they fit properly.

Kosmas takes the money.

KOSMAS: I'll come to see her on the weekend.

His father looks at him.

KOSMAS: Grandma.

FATHER: Are you crazy?

KOSMAS: Why?

FATHER: Because the day before yesterday they took three men from Elato. And all the boys your age in the village are sleeping out in the fields at night.[8]

The assistant jumps deftly down from the roof of the bus. The bus starts moving.

ASSISTANT: We're leaving, Dimitris.

He goes and slams shut one of the doors.

The father gets on the bus. The bus slowly backs up. Kosmas steps aside. One of the back windows is pulled down and reveals the father's head. He is saying something to Kosmas. Kosmas does not have time to answer. The assistant steps between them, jumps onto the bus pulling the door shut behind him, and the bus begins to move out. Kosmas, motionless, watches it pull away.

8. Kosmas is here warned by his father to keep a low profile to avoid being snatched by the rebels, who continued to recruit unwilling participants in the communist insurgency even as the government carried out its cleanup operations.

5.

Nikos's rented room with high ceiling.[9] To one side is a large dormer window. The afternoon light soft through the curtains. Very little furniture. A bed, a simple wooden table with schoolbooks on it. A brazier in the corner with a few coals burning. On top of the table a chair has been placed. Nikos is standing on the chair. With the upper part of the curtains slightly open, he is peering discreetly outside. On the terrace opposite them, closed in by a parapet, is a low, covered laundry shed. The pane in its only small window is fogged over with steam. On a taut wire for hanging clothes are a few forgotten clothespins. A small bird alights for a while on the wire, then flies off. Nikos watches obstinately, lost in thought. His musings are cut short by the sound of the doorbell. He turns toward the sound, taking care not to lose his balance on the chair, and listens. From further back the sound of the entrance door opening can be heard. A boy's voice asking something; a woman's voice grunting a one-word reply from above. Then, footsteps ascending the stairs. Nikos waits motionless. The footsteps in the small hallway draw near and stop. A knock on his door. He bends forward, careful not to make any noise.

NIKOS: Who's there?
– Kosmas.
NIKOS: Wait a second.

9. In the 1940s many Greek towns and villages did not have high schools, and it was customary for students from these villages to attend high school in the nearest big city. Both Nikos, whose village Alonistaina was too far away from the capital, and Kosmas, whose unspecified village was also too far away, consequently rented rooms to be able to attend high school.

He climbs down onto the table, then from the table to the floor. He unbolts the door and opens it slightly, blocking the opening with his body. He sees Kosmas by himself. He steps to the side, lets him in and re-bolts the door. Kosmas, seeing the chair on top of the table, is taken aback.

KOSMAS: What's going on?
NIKOS: Shhhh . . . !
KOSMAS: The army captain's woman?

Nikos motions him to be quiet. He deftly climbs back up to his post. Kosmas takes off his coat, throws it on the bed and gets up on the table. They do not both fit on the chair. He tries to open the curtain a bit more.

NIKOS: No, not the curtain.
KOSMAS: What's she doing?
NIKOS: She's bathing.
KOSMAS: Can you see her?
NIKOS: Not yet.
KOSMAS: So?

Nikos doesn't answer. He is focused on the scene across. He soon bursts out with a muted exclamation.

NIKOS: There she is.

On the terrace, the small, warped, wooden door of the laundry shed opens, pushed from inside. The army captain's woman appears, about thirty years old, with hidden curves, a simple beauty. Her hair pulled up high, wrapped in a towel. Wearing a double-breasted, heavy bathrobe with the sleeves rolled up, she places a basin with washed underwear and shirts on the parapet. With a damp cloth she begins wiping the wire. As she moves sideways, the motion of her knees pushes her bathrobe open every so often, revealing the shape of her bare thighs. Kosmas, excited, tries to climb up on the chair next to Nikos.

KOSMAS: Move over a little.
NIKOS: We'll fall.

Just in time he grabs onto a dead wire protruding from the wall on his left. They manage to retain their balance for a while longer. The army captain's woman takes the basin and puts it in front of her, below the tautly-drawn wire. She bends down, pulls up a piece of clothing, shakes it out, stands on tiptoes, hangs it up; then, before she bends over a second time, she looks around, quickly undoes her bathrobe, and ties it again even tighter. With this most stirring revelation, and as Nikos tries to change hands, the center of gravity shifts, and amidst the racket of the chair tumbling down they find themselves in a heap on the floor. They do not move or speak for a moment. Nikos looks at Kosmas, feeling relieved.

NIKOS: Did you break anything?
KOSMAS: No.

Kosmas moves and finds a more comfortable position on the floor, squatting, looking between his legs at his pants rising into a small tent-like mound.

NIKOS: Not that either?

Kosmas, silent, slowly shakes his head no. Outside, from the end of the hallway, hesitant footsteps can be heard approaching.

Then a woman's voice.

– Niko, what happened, boy?

Nikos bites his lip to keep from laughing.

NIKOS: It was just a few books that fell off the shelves, Madame Aliki.

Holding his breath, he waits for her footsteps to recede. Then he jumps up, returns the fallen chair to its place, tucks his shirt into his pants and, coming up behind Kosmas, pokes his knee into his back.

NIKOS: Get up.
KOSMAS: What do you have in mind?
NIKOS: Nothing.
KOSMAS: Why did you disappear this morning?
NIKOS: I had things to do.

Kosmas looks at him puzzled.

NIKOS: I can't tell you. But next time I'll take you with me.

Kosmas gets up. He goes to the window.

KOSMAS: Can I open the curtain now?

Without waiting for an answer he pushes it open. The afternoon light floods the room. Kosmas stands there looking at the wall across the way. The parapet on the terrace precludes any view. Hanging on the tightly-drawn wire are shirts and women's underwear. Distant reflections from the sun splinter on a windowpane somewhere. The bell of a passing bicycle is heard in the street below. Nikos stoops over the brazier and carefully covers the coal with ashes.

NIKOS: What happened with the French teacher?
KOSMAS: Who told you about that?

He puts on his coat.

NIKOS: Michalis did. He stopped by after school was out.
KOSMAS: She kept me after class, for ten minutes.
NIKOS: To punish you?

There is an ironic tone to his voice. They go out to the hallway. Kosmas laughs.

KOSMAS: Just an excuse to be alone with me.

Nikos locks up.

NIKOS: What did she say to you?
KOSMAS: That I draw nicely.

They walk through the hallway. The right side is all windows. The balconies on the buildings across are deserted. They go downstairs and out to the street.

NIKOS: And what about the "Triangle of Death"?
KOSMAS: She asked me if I had ever seen one.
NIKOS: And what did you answer?
KOSMAS: That I haven't.
NIKOS: Good for you. You get an A-plus for honesty.

Kosmas stops. He looks around, then glances confidentially at Nikos.

KOSMAS: And then, standing in front of the blackboard, she began to slowly pull her skirt up. She looked at me without speaking, with a soft, mysterious smile. Then her thighs were showing and her garter belt and the bare flesh under it. She had nothing else on, and her triangle was perfect, brown and curly, and she stayed like that for a minute with her eyes closed to let me admire her beauty unhindered. Then she let her skirt fall all at once. "Mine is the Triangle of Life," she said. "On the first night of the new moon I'll be expecting you at my house."

Nikos applauds.

NIKOS: When will there be a new moon?

Kosmas laughs.

6.

A military ambulance is crossing the main street. Preceded by a motorcycle. Kosmas and Nikos watch it move away. Then they prepare to cross the street. On the sidewalk, outside a general supply and wholesale store, their classmate, Yiannis, wearing a brimmed cap. He is loading parcels with packs of cigarettes onto the grille of his bicycle. He sees them.

YIANNIS: Out for a ride?

NIKOS: Yep.

YIANNIS: What did you do about the homework?

KOSMAS: It's still sitting there stewing.

Yiannis goes into the shop. He comes back out immediately. He gets on his bike. The other two cross the street and walk toward the small street above it, intending to turn there. With two swift jams on the pedal he catches up to them. He picks up their pace and follows them. Nikos looks at his cap.

NIKOS: Why are you wearing that?

YIANNIS: For tactical reasons.

KOSMAS: The studious, hard-working schoolboy.

YIANNIS: Exactly.

KOSMAS: Is the old man at least paying you for your work?

YIANNIS: No, but at least I don't have to listen to him bitching about feeding me. At my age he was supporting his widowed mother and his sister.

KOSMAS: I see.

YIANNIS: Lampsanos is preparing snap exams for tomorrow.

NIKOS: Where did you hear that?
YIANNIS: Cross your heart.
– And hope to die.
YIANNIS: From the Parrot. He's tutoring him privately.
KOSMAS: Why, that son-of-a-bitch . . .
YIANNIS: Don't let this get out.

He starts pedaling again, gets up speed, and zipping around the curve, disappears at the next corner.

NIKOS: I think we should make the most of this information.

7.

From somewhere far away the sound of a chainsaw. A small square. A few small dusty trees. An equally dusty kiosk. Further on, the bicycle shop. Koularmanis on the sidewalk sitting on his low wooden stool in front of a tub with dirty water. Next to him several tires for repair.

KOULARMANIS: Hey, give me that.

He takes the bladder of a soccer ball from a ten- or twelve-year-old boy standing next to him and looks it over. Then he puts it to his mouth and begins to blow it up. Kosmas and Nikos appear around the corner. They walk toward him.

– Hi Nikolas.

Koularmanis with the soccer ball bladder in his mouth and his cheeks puffed up does not reply. The two boys go inside. They are familiar with the place. They pick up a few suspender clips for their pants from the counter, glancing at the bicycles for rent. Some other bicycles have been placed against a wall along the sidewalk. Koularmanis has submerged the soccer ball bladder in the tub and is silently watching the bubbles of air shooting up to the surface. Kosmas selects a bicycle, pulls it onto the street, tests the brakes. Nikos does the same.

The door of the kiosk opens and the one-armed kiosk-owner appears.

KIOSK-OWNER: Nikolas.

Everyone turns in his direction. On the other side of the square a wagon loaded with about ten, probably more, hastily assembled empty coffins.

Everyone stops to look toward it. An old lady passing by has also stopped. The momentary silence is broken by the noise of shutters opening suddenly in the house across the way. Koularmanis stands up with the inflated bladder in his hand. A gray-haired man leans out the window across the way. He is wearing a white doctor's gown.

GRAY-HAIRED MAN: Did they bring them?
KIOSK-OWNER: They did.
GRAY-HAIRED MAN: How many?
KIOSK-OWNER: Fourteen.

Someone comes over to the kiosk for cigarettes. The owner goes inside. The doctor watches the wagon moving away for a while and goes back inside. The old lady continues on her way, silently making the sign of the cross. Koularmanis turns back toward the tub. He blows the bladder up again, submerges it in the water, and taking a thick purple copy pencil from his ear, marks the hole with a circle. Kosmas and Nikos walk over to him with their bicycles.

NIKOS: Who did they bring?
KOULARMANIS: The dead from Monodendri.

He lets the air out of the ball, takes a patch, and begins rubbing it with a piece of sandpaper.

KOSMAS: It's ten past four, Nikolas.

Koularmanis looks inside at the old alarm clock hanging on the wall.

KOULARMANIS: OK.

He gets up, goes inside and notes down the check-out time. Kosmas and Nikos get on their bicycles, make a U-turn and leave.

The sun is descending in the west. Kosmas and Nikos on their bicycles. Moving at a steady pace. They turn at an uphill stretch, begin pedaling harder, reach the top and disappear behind it.

8.

Back side of hill. At the bottom of the hill a huge vacant lot with clusters of trees all around. Nikos and Kosmas go racing toward it. Flying along as though they were freed from gravity. When they reach the bottom they separate. One goes in one direction, the other in the opposite direction. On the eastern side of the vacant lot a cement gallows, high and very long, holding up a water pipe. As he reaches it Kosmas brakes suddenly and stops. He plants his feet on the ground and watches Nikos, who continues completing a circle around the vacant lot. Then he pulls up next to Kosmas, braking just as suddenly. Further away, a couple disappears in the cluster of trees. Kosmas raises his head and sniffs the air.

KOSMAS: Smells like human flesh to me.

Nikos smiles. From a distance the sound of a church bell tolling in mourning. Kosmas turns decisively toward Nikos.

KOSMAS: Shall we head over there?
NIKOS: Let's go.

They climb onto their bicycles. They ride off.

9.

Railroad tracks. Next to them a single fenced-in house. The brothel. Further west the buildings of the Railroad Station. Behind it, on the side where the "Ice-cream & Spaghetti" confectioners is located but hidden from view, the rhythmic hum of its engines working makes itself heard. In front of the railroad tracks are several bald patches of land that have been turned into a makeshift soccer field. A vacant lot. Further along, the cemetery. Behind the high surrounding stone wall, between the outlines of the cypress trees, one can make out the church. And also several marble crosses from graves. The large iron gate to the yard is open. The military ambulance is parked in a corner, closed. They are lowering the last coffins from the wagon and putting them in the ambulance. The wagon leaves. An armed sentry at the entrance, bayonet affixed. Kosmas and Nikos reach a small mound in the middle of the surrounding fields. They get off their bicycles and watch. They guess more than see what is going on inside the gate. Nikos nudges Kosmas. A young woman is crossing the vacant lot. On the railroad tracks a low open personnel conveyor moves toward the station. The workers with their feet hanging out also watch the woman walking slowly, as in a ritual, toward the cemetery.

KOSMAS: I saw her early this afternoon. In the horse-and-buggy.

He continues.

KOSMAS: Every Tuesday they go to the doctor's. All of them. They go there, they spread their legs for him, and he examines them.

NIKOS: The "Africana" too?

Kosmas nods his head affirmatively.

The woman, quite far away now, goes past them. She is holding a small pillow in her hands and an armful of flowers.

KOSMAS: Do you know where they use those pillows?

Nikos looks at him.

KOSMAS: They put them under their hips. To keep from getting tired.

They stop talking and watch the woman. She is walking along the white cement wall. She approaches the sentry. The sentry smiles at her with a conspiratorial air and lets her pass.

NIKOS: Let's go over there too.

They walk toward the church.

SENTRY: It's forbidden.
KOSMAS: We just want to have a look.

The sentry looks at them.

SENTRY: OK, go have a look and then clear out.

They go inside.

10.

Piled against the wall in the direction of the cypress trees are fourteen stretchers. The "Africana" is the last one there. Four other Mary Magdalenes from the fenced-in house have arrived before her. These women, following the age-old tradition of their profession, have washed the dead soldiers' faces and wailed over them. And the heads of all the soldiers are resting on small, soft pillows.

DAY TWO

11.

The classroom. Silence. The students bent over their notebooks. The teacher monitoring from his desk. Nikos looks toward Yiannis in the other row of desks. Yiannis winks at him: We pulled it off. Nikos gives Kosmas next to him a nudge.

NIKOS: Get up.
KOSMAS: What are you up to now?

Nikos takes out his cup from under his desk and stands up. He is the first one. The teacher looks at him in disbelief. In a low tone of voice.

TEACHER: Are you finished?
NIKOS: Yes, Sir.
TEACHER: Give me your exam paper.

Nikos walks forward and gives it to him. The teacher examines it. Somewhat surprised, he turns and looks at Nikos.

NIKOS: May I leave the room, Sir?
TEACHER: Is it urgent?
NIKOS: Yes, Sir.

12.

Cloudy weather. In the inner courtyard. Beneath the metal awning the woman in charge prepares milk in two large cauldrons. Nikos walks down the cement stairway. He stops where it turns at the landing. Through the windows of the classroom on the ground floor — plastered halfway up by a thick layer of paint — he can see the students' backs and at her desk the young French teacher.

He stands there for a while watching her. The sound of a door opening is heard from the floor below. Nikos is startled. He continues descending the stairs. At the bottom he runs into the principal.

PRINCIPAL: You, what are you doing here?
NIKOS: We had a test, Sir.
PRINCIPAL: And you're finished?
NIKOS: Yes, Sir.
PRINCIPAL: Did you do well?
NIKOS: I finished, Sir.

Formal questions with a conventional stern overtone.

The principal ascends the stairs. Nikos moves toward the lavatories. He pushes open a door. While he is urinating he looks at various innocent bits of graffiti on the walls. The most risqué is a sketch of a woman in an indecent pose.

He comes back out. The woman in charge has disappeared. Nikos slowly walks toward the half-painted windows of the ground-floor classroom. He finds a small opening and presses his eye to it. The backs of students and the French teacher at her desk. After a while he turns his head back to look around and make sure that no one can see him, and again presses his eye to the opening. The students' backs are no longer in view and the teacher, as though she knows that he is watching her, is turned in his direction. For a second she smiles at him silently. Then she begins to slowly tug her skirt upward. Before her knees are even revealed the bell rings for a break. Nikos jumps back. On the first balcony the woman in charge stops ringing the bell and disappears inside. It is quiet for a while. Then a door opens. Then another one. The stairs fill with boys. They run about. Pandemonium. The Gym teacher blows his whistle. The classes line up for the doling out of the morning snack. Several other teachers watch. Snack time begins. One of the teachers supervises next to the cauldrons. Nikos, Kosmas, and Yiannis are talking. There is always some impetus behind them spurring them on.

KOSMAS: There are no classes after this.
YIANNIS: Why not?
KOSMAS: We're all supposed to go to the Cathedral.
NIKOS: For the funeral?
KOSMAS: Yes.
YIANNIS: What do you say?

He looks at them knowingly. The gym teacher interrupts them.

GYM TEACHER: Time to go, let's go.

13.

The door of the empty classroom opens with a push toward the inside. Nikos enters hurriedly. He collects the books and the caps — his and Kosmas's — from their desks. And also Yiannis's books and cap from his desk. He moves adroitly back out, goes downstairs and discreetly slips out onto the street. Further along his two friends are waiting for him. He gives them their things, takes Kosmas's cup from him and just as they are turning the corner they run into their Greek literature teacher. They stop suddenly. Nikos, who is taking his first sip, almost chokes.

GREEK LIT. TEACHER: Alexopoulos, Danakas, Granias.

All three are left speechless and embarrassed.

GREEK LIT. TEACHER: Where are you going in such a hurry?

He tears the wrapping paper from a package of cigarettes that he has just bought. Forty years old, he doesn't look at all like a teacher.

YIANNIS: Over there, Sir.
GREEK LIT. TEACHER: Not for cigarettes, of course.
YIANNIS: For pencils, Sir.

The Greek literature teacher looks at them with a slightly ironic smile.

GREEK LIT. TEACHER: Alright, then. I want the three of you back inside with your pencils.

He goes out, leaving them standing there staring at each other, trapped.

14.

Cloudy weather. From an invisible defective loudspeaker the funeral mass can be heard faintly. In the town square, in front of the Cathedral, people stand motionless. Small new groups of people continue to file in silently and reverently. The schools, in loosely-assembled formations, have been lined up in the streets around the square. The boys' class split into small groups of friends. Across from them the Girls' High School. Nikos is staring in that direction. A girl has cut class and disappeared under the arcades. Yiannis, following Nikos's gaze, whispers jokingly.

YIANNIS: Dust to dust. Ashes to ashes.

The girl disappears in the crowd. There is a strange, muted atmosphere of reflection. The Greek literature teacher comes over to the boys. He has lit a cigarette and is smoking it guardedly. From the loudspeaker the voice of the priest is heard twice over. His words are hard to make out, but the well-known and familiar psalming makes their meaning clear. Kosmas leans toward the Greek literature teacher.

KOSMAS: Do you believe all that, Sir?

GREEK LIT. TEACHER: Believe what?

KOSMAS: Listen.

GREEK LIT. TEACHER: This is poetry of an extraordinarily high level.

KOSMAS: I didn't mean if you believed those words as poetry.

GREEK LIT. TEACHER: As what, then?

KOSMAS: As a perspective.

GREEK LIT. TEACHER: A perspective for whom?

KOSMAS: For everyone. Especially for the people inside.

GREEK LIT. TEACHER: I can only speak for myself.

The conversation is calm, with voices kept low. Several more students have gathered around them.

KOSMAS: But that's avoiding the question.

GREEK LIT. TEACHER: Perhaps. But in certain cases there is no other way.

A fine, imperceptible drizzle begins. The Greek literature teacher spots the French teacher a bit further along opening her umbrella.

He tosses his cigarette butt away, smiles at them and goes off toward the French teacher. In the meantime the psalming has stopped and there is a soundless interval. Then a repetitive blowing into the defective loudspeaker and someone immediately begins delivering a eulogy. The transmission is bad, most of the words are lost. Their grandiose oratory fills the air. The rain grows stronger, many more umbrellas now open. Some people move under the arcades to protect themselves. The sound of a bass drum booms forth like a signal. Various officials have begun to file out of the Cathedral. Several military commands crack through the air. The teachers begin reassembling their classes. Nikos takes one last hurried look around him. He locates Kosmas. They exchange glances.

15.

Nikos sneaks out cautiously and loses himself in the crowd. He reaches the westernmost arcade and stops under a baroque-looking metal awning. Just across from him a barbershop, a sign on its door-pane forbidding soldiers to enter. As he waits for Kosmas he watches the barber lathering the face of a customer. From the direction of the cathedral a band begins playing the funeral march and slowly moving away as the drizzle grows stronger. Soon it has become a heavy rainfall.

16.

A wet, deserted balcony with neoclassical cast iron railings and marble balcony cantilevers. The glass door-panes fogged over in the intensifying rain. Distant sounds of music. Behind the drapes, drawn and flapping like a curtain falling, the indistinct figure of a young girl.

17.

The countryside. The rain continues, but a spring rain, gentle and sunlit. Nikos is crossing a wheat field strewn with poppies. At the top of a hill there is a small, deserted house. He approaches it and slowly circles round it. It is completely shuttered. He stops, discouraged, and looks down toward the other side of the hill. A window opens behind him. He turns toward it. From the window the French teacher looks at him silently and rather sternly.

FRENCH TEACHER: You're late.
NIKOS: I had to get rid of Kosmas.

He stands before her uneasy and somewhat exposed in the fine silver rain. He looks at the closed door. As though she had understood what he was thinking, she says,

FRENCH TEACHER: The door is broken.
NIKOS: How did you get in?
FRENCH TEACHER: From the roof.

She shows him a portable wooden ladder sitting in a corner that he had not noticed earlier, when he was circling the house.

FRENCH TEACHER: Don't just stand there, because they'll see you.

Nikos moves hesitantly toward the ladder. The French teacher stops him.

FRENCH TEACHER: I think it's easier through here. Give me your hand.

She leans out and takes hold of his hand.

FRENCH TEACHER: Put your foot there. And be careful not to hit your head up above.

With one sudden strong tug, Nikos is up on the window. From there he easily jumps inside.

The inside of the house is completely different from what anyone could have imagined. Part of the roof has collapsed halfway. The remaining portion is supported by bare rough-planed rafters. The whole place looks a bit like a tobacco warehouse. The French teacher closes the one-piece window shutter, bolts it from inside and stands facing him. Nikos notices for the first time that she is wearing a Greek schoolgirl's uniform.

FRENCH TEACHER: And you've been saying bad things about me to Kosmas.

Nikos is confused. He tries to make an excuse.

NIKOS: No, there must be some misunderstanding. I swear it.

FRENCH TEACHER: Stop lying. And stop speaking to me so formally.

In the opposite corner there is a rocking chair with a cushion on it. The French teacher takes an old worn-out broom and sweeps a part of the floor next to the rocking chair. She takes off her school uniform and spreads it carefully on the floor. She is left wearing her sweater and skirt. She sits on the laid-out uniform and remains motionless for a while, with her arms locked around her knees. Then she lies back and, supporting herself on her elbows, pulls up her skirt. Surprised, she looks at Nikos, who continues to stand in place without moving.

FRENCH TEACHER: Why are you just standing there?

Nikos moves slowly toward her, like a sleepwalker, and avoids staring at her bare skin. It's just as Kosmas has described her, plus the black underwear. Awkwardly and timidly, he stands over her not knowing what to do. His inexperience touches her.

FRENCH TEACHER: Sit down here next to me.

Nikos obeys. The French teacher takes the cushion from the rocking chair, places it under her hips with almost professional agility and lies completely back with her eyes closed.

FRENCH TEACHER: Can you hear the rain on the roof-tiles?

Nikos turns and looks at her without answering. Her closed eyes embolden him. On her lips a delightful, inviting smile appears. He reaches out his hand and shyly places it between her thighs. His head feels ready to explode. His hand moves further upward, then feels around everywhere. He presses his face against her chest. Her scent excites him. He tries to pull down her panties without success. He keeps trying but with no result, even though she herself moves her body around to make it easier for him. His anguish now peaks. Possessed by the same anguish, the French teacher draws her panties violently aside and tears them off. At the crucial moment, the revelation of her curly womanly bush dazzles Nikos. In the perfect silence that now prevails, nothing but the rain on the roof-tiles is audible.

18.

Nikos turns on the small lamp on the night table next to him and sits up in his bed, unexpectedly awakened and morose. He remains motionless for a short while but the room is cold and he begins to shiver. He throws his covers off resolutely, takes a pair of underpants from his old cardboard suitcase and goes out to the hallway. He goes into the bathroom, takes off his moist underpants, wets a towel and washes his private parts. The cold water awakens him fully. He dries himself, puts on the new underpants and goes back into the hallway. He only now realizes that a new day is dawning. Half-naked and barefoot, he stands for a while staring out at the gray, rainy morning. On the roof-tiles the same restrained sound of the night rain can be heard.

α. Ο πατέρας π

βιαστικός, με

ήσαν σήμερα.

κείο. Δίνει στ

λευθερώσει τα

DAY THREE

19.

The rain has stopped, but the atmosphere continues to be damp and gray. From the windows of the dairy shop the morning traffic on the road is visible. From a stove pipe across the way, curls of smoke flutter out. Nikos, his elbows resting on a small marble table, is holding a half-empty glass of milk in both hands. He is still lost in thought and sullen — in fact he is still under the influence of his unrealized dream. At the next table the following dialogue can be heard:

– What time did they take Ilias?

– At three in the morning. Eleni woke up to open the door and almost fell over. Almost had a heart attack.

– Did they send them off?

– Not yet. The train from Kalamata is on its way. They're waiting for the men from Sparta, won't they take any men from Sparta?

– How many men did they take from here?

– They say about two hundred. No one knows yet.

– Will they let people give them things?

– Why shouldn't they? A change of clothes, a shirt. They can't take them like that, can they?

The door opens and a young girl walks in. Flustered and in a hurry, she goes over to the two men who are talking next to Nikos. She is carrying a package under her arm.

GIRL: Good-morning, Uncle.

– Good-morning, my girl, do you want to sit down?

GIRL: No, Uncle.

– You want something to drink?

GIRL: No, Uncle, we haven't time.

The uncle gets to his feet. He tries to take out some money. The other man doesn't let him.

– Get going, Dimitris. Off you go.

They leave. The girl walks ahead of them, she opens the door and steps aside so her uncle can go out first.

Nikos empties his glass and puts it down on the marble tabletop. He looks toward the waiter. On the wall a pendulum clock strikes the half hour. Seven-thirty. The sound, soft and faint, slowly dies down. The man from the next table gets up, walks toward the back, and goes into the restroom. The waiter places a warm cream-filled pastry in front of Nikos. Nikos pays, he silently consumes the pastry with a brisk, steady rhythm, he stands up, he puts on his cap, he takes his books from the chair next to him, and he leaves.

20.

Unusual activity outside the high school. Groups of students coming in, others leaving. Kosmas and a few other boys cross paths with Nikos, who arrives there innocently enough.

NIKOS: What's up?
KOSMAS: There's no school.
APOSTOLIS: The Special Mountain Combat Forces took over the high school building.
NIKOS: When?
APOSTOLIS: Last night.
NIKOS: And now what?
KOSMAS: School is at the Girls' High School. Us in the morning, the girls in the afternoon.
NIKOS: Who said so?
KOSMAS: Kremmydas is here. They put up notices.
APOSTOLIS: Today in particular, because it was unexpected, we'll go in the afternoon.
NIKOS: And how long will this go on?
APOSTOLIS: Indefinitely.
KOSMAS: No one said anything. No one knows.
NIKOS: Let's go find out.

He takes them back again. They approach from a short distance. At the gate of the high school, a sentry with nothing but a pistol. In the courtyard, from what can be seen, men are moving around, some half-naked with towels over their shoulders and unlaced boots, others holding paper cups with hot drinks. In the corners, desks piled up from the emptied-out classrooms. Next to the sentry the teacher, Mr. Kremmydas, intermittently giving out information to the children approaching him or pointing them to a handwritten notice posted on a wall. A jeep arrives and stops at the entrance. A young major gets out. A first lieutenant follows him. The sentry greets them casually. They go inside. The jeep waits with its motor running.

MIHALIS: That must be their commander.

APOSTOLIS: Do you know what those stripes on his sleeve mean? Six months on the front lines.

On one of the balconies a door opens, a sergeant steps out and leaning downward shouts.

SERGEANT: Despotopoulos. Despotopoulos.

He gets no reply and goes back inside. Apostolis suggests they leave.

MIHALIS: Either they just carried out operations or they're about to carry out operations.

They begin to move away. Nikos addresses Kosmas:

NIKOS: Where's Yiannis?

KOSMAS: He hasn't shown up yet.

APOSTOLIS: They arrested his father.

– What?

APOSTOLIS: Didn't you hear about it? They were arresting people during the night. They're deporting them as informants.

MIHALIS: That's why that notice was on the door of his shop.

NIKOS: That's nonsense.

APOSTOLIS: Anyone got a cigarette?

KOSMAS: No one.

21.

They go around the corner. Ahead of them are two other students. Nikos shouts.

NIKOS: Vangelis.

They stop and wait for them. They join with the others into a single new group and continue on their way, some walking in front, some lagging behind.

Nikos to Vangelis.

NIKOS: Did you finish it?

VANGELIS: Not yet.

NIKOS: What do you think of it?

VANGELIS: Did you think I'd have trouble reading it, the way you've underlined the whole book?

NIKOS: Did you get to the scene with the widow?[10]

VANGELIS: Yes.

NIKOS: Isn't it amazing?

VANGELIS: I preferred the part where he says that he cut off his finger because it got in his way when he was potting.

NIKOS: That's a strong scene too.

VANGELIS: What did Vogaris say? Did you talk about it?

NIKOS: He annoyed me a bit.

10. The reference is from a book well-known at the time to our protagonists: Nikos Kazantzakis's *Bios kai politia tou Alexi Zorba (The Life and Times of Alexis Zorbas),* Athens, Dimitrakos Publishers, 1946. This deeply existential book was translated into numerous languages before it was made into the Oscar-winning movie "Zorba the Greek" in 1964 under the direction of Michalis Kakoyannis, with music by Mikis Theodorakis, and actors Anthony Quinn, Alan Bates, and Irene Pappas.

Vangelis looks at him. Nikos apes the teacher.

NIKOS: "There is an imperceptible but formidable difference between inspired writing and bombastic writing."

Vangelis laughs.

They come out at the far end of the large, empty square. Both its sides, eastern and northern, fenced in by parks. Apostolis, in the lead, stops at the kiosk on the corner and buys a few loose cigarettes. Everyone gathers round him.

APOSTOLIS: Cigarette, anyone?
MIHALIS: Me.

None of the others move. Apostolis waves the cigarettes in front of them.

APOSTOLIS: Vangelis, Dimitris?

They refuse. He gives one to Mihalis, he puts another in his mouth and the rest in his shirt pocket inside his sweater. With a showy movement he takes a lighter out of his back pants pocket and rolls out its long wick with the same flair. He lights it, he gently blows on the lighted tip of the wick and gives Mihalis a light.

APOSTOLIS: Here you are, my child.

Next he lights up himself. A portable loudspeaker that is just beginning to be audible slightly spoils his performance.

Everyone's attention turns in that direction. As the voice draws near, the words become clearer.

– Tonight and for four more days at the Apollo Cinema Theater, the troupe of the well-known variety leading ladies Iró Handá and Toúla Drákou in a special collaboration with all the best numbers from this year's season, tonight and for four more days . . .

A small car comes into the square and stops. As the announcement program continues, two men emerge from the car, take down from the grille on its roof a two-piece folding placard with promotional photographs of the troupe — with flesh exposed as was the fashion at the time — and they set it up at the far end of the square. They get back in and the car pulls away with its loudspeaker still on. The boys walk over to the sign. For a while they admire the beauty of the female members of the troupe in the photographs. From the other end of the square, on the road between the two parks, two women appear. They are wearing identical scotch-plaid skirts fastened with safety pins, identical sweaters, identical coats.

Kosmas sees them first. He nudges Mihalis.

KOSMAS: The "twins."

Michalis looks toward them.

MIHALIS: Oh, my God.

Dreamily, he takes a puff from his cigarette and loses himself staring at them. Others are now focusing their attention on the twins. The nearer they get, the more obvious the twins' age difference becomes. One is under forty, the other under twenty.

APOSTOLIS: Well, I prefer the mother.
KOSMAS: You pervert.
NIKOS: I'll take the mother and the daughter.

Vangelis tries to say something, but no one pays any attention to him. Dimitris, silent, is slowly seething inside. Walking along, the women reach the same spot on the opposite pavement.

MIHALIS: They really are "twins." How old do you think she was when she had her?

NIKOS: If she's thirty-five now, maybe she was eighteen.

Just before they turn at the next corner, the younger one looks over toward them and smiles at them timidly.

KOSMAS: There they are, look.
APOSTOLIS: Imagine a threesome with those two.

He has no time to finish his sentence. Dimitris punches him twice in the face. Apostolis is taken by surprise. In his attempts to react, he drops his books and his cup. Dimitris takes advantage of this and punches him again several times. Vangelis tries to come between them and push Dimitris away. The other boys are at a complete loss. Apostolis recovers and goes on the attack to take revenge. He comes to grips with Dimitris. Vangelis, between them, receives the most punches. The other boys step in to separate them. Vangelis and Kosmas pull Dimitris, still silent, away. Apostolis, immobilized by Mihalis and Nikos, swears and makes threats. His eye is already swollen, and blood is running from cuts on his lips. Nikos bends down, picks up Apostolis's books and his cup and puts them in his hands. Several passersby, who had stopped while the fight was in progress, continue on their way. Vangelis and Dimitris have disappeared around the corner. Kosmas comes back from there. As suddenly as the quarrel began, it ends. Apostolis wipes his mouth with the back of his hand.

APOSTOLIS: That asshole, what's wrong with him? If I see him again, I'll beat the shit out of him.

KOSMAS: What are you talking about, jerk; what can you expect when she's his mother's sister and her daughter is his first cousin.

This information makes quite an impression. For a while there is silence.

NIKOS: Who said so?

KOSMAS: Vangelis.

Apostolis loses control.

APOSTOLIS: And how was I supposed to know that? By looking in my crystal ball?

MIHALIS: Well, now that you do know, cut it out.

APOSTOLIS: Oh, fuck!

He looks at the others.

APOSTOLIS: Did he do any damage to me?

MIHALIS: Nothing serious.

APOSTOLIS: Nothing serious, but my eye is bashed practically closed.

He spits and wipes his mouth again.

APOSTOLIS: And what should I tell them at home?

KOSMAS: You've got time for that, you'll figure it out.

MIHALIS: Are you staying?

NIKOS: Yes.

APOSTOLIS: You think this is funny, man?

NIKOS: (*to Mihalis*) Why don't you take him to the pharmacy and have them put on a few band-aids.

Apostolis shoves his hand in the shirt-pocket under his sweater and takes out whatever cigarettes are left, all crumbled up.

APOSTOLIS: Well, there go my cigarettes.

He tosses them away. Mihalis takes him by the arm.

MIHALIS: Shall we go?

The two of them start out.

MIHALIS: Are you all staying?

NIKOS: Yes.

MIHALIS: What time is school this afternoon?

KOSMAS: At two.

MIHALIS: See you.
– Bye.

The cathedral clock is heard striking nine o'clock. Nearby the sound of a truck putting on its brakes. Nikos and Kosmas turn toward it. At the steps of the courthouse, which is located on the upper side of the square, four village women clad in black have gathered. Two grey-haired old men accompany them. From the closed personnel carrier truck that has stopped in front of them, eight armed guards emerge. Behind them in handcuffs three young men, scrawny but freshly-shaved in ties and cheap suits. The guards push them quickly inside, keeping those waiting to see them from getting near them.

NIKOS: (*looking in that direction*) Shall we go see?

22.

Nikos and Kosmas climb the marble staircase inside the courthouse. The steps are worn from use. They stop in the center of the large high-ceilinged lobby to get their bearings. Clerks are coming and going, all kinds of people, law enforcement officers. A tall imposing fifty-year old man who seems to be from the capitol steps out of the lawyers' office. He is accompanied by an assistant. They watch him as he enters one of the courtrooms.

KOSMAS: Who's that?

Without realizing it, he lowers his voice to a whisper. Nikos does the same.

NIKOS: They bring lawyers from Athens. The local lawyers won't take them on.

KOSMAS: Why not?

Nikos shrugs his shoulders.

From some distance away they see the inner door behind the judge's bench open and the military judges appear in full uniform. The accused men and the audience rise. A gendarme at the entrance stops the boys.

GENDARME: Are you relatives?

NIKOS: No.

The gendarme looks at them with their caps and the books in their hands.

GENDARME: What are you boys doing here? Why don't you run along and do your homework?

He turns his back on them and takes up his position again. At ease, his hands behind him. Forehead toward the bench. Nikos and Kosmas move back self-consciously. They turn to leave. Behind the half-open door of a narrow room, they see a wizened woman of a certain age with glasses bent over a typewriter, tapping on the keys, completely wrapped up in what she is doing as though it was the most important thing in the world.

23.

They go outside. Nikos pauses on a wide landing. The sky is still cloudy.

NIKOS: The other day no one told me anything.

KOSMAS: (*drawing his own conclusions*) So that's why you ran out. You came here.

They go down to the street.

NIKOS: Someone from our village was on trial.

KOSMAS: How long did he get?

NIKOS: Two consecutive life sentences. Arson and homicide.

KOSMAS: What did he do?

NIKOS: His first cousins. They burned their house with their blind grandmother inside. According to the witnesses. There were also some other offenses . . .

NIKOS: "Consecutive" is pretty funny, eh? Imagine executing them by firing squad and then lining them up against the wall again.

NIKOS: A one-off penalty. Maybe they're saving the second consecutive sentence for the next life.

KOSMAS: Shall we go find Yiannis?

NIKOS: Will he be at the shop?

KOSMAS: If he's there. Who would have thought his father was a communist?

NIKOS: And why would he necessarily be one? Just because they arrested him?

24.

A small church squeezed between two narrow streets. The courtyard freshly scrubbed and next to its open door a small candelabrum filled with lighted wax candles. A woman further back is rubbing and polishing the bronze vessels. Nikos and Kosmas pass by. A long high stone wall extends from the church. Behind it the tops of cypress trees and other greenery in bloom, a vague, mysterious setting, seeing as the inside of the garden is not clearly in view. At the far end of the stone wall a one-story stone house. The shutters on the windows facing the street are closed. Smoke comes out of a stove pipe on the side where the garden is. They change pace.

KOSMAS: Imagine if she's inside.
NIKOS: Well, there's smoke coming from the stove.
KOSMAS: But not from her.

Nikos looks at him.

KOSMAS: It must be Vogaris.
NIKOS: Vogaris only visits at night. And not every night.
KOSMAS: Did they really see him coming out of there at dawn?
NIKOS: Ask Nikolaou yourself.
KOSMAS: Where does he live?
NIKOS: Near the sign.

He shows him a two-story house diagonally across from them. On the railing of the balcony there is an old, faded sign: "Christos Nikolaou. Chemist. Enologist."

They arrive in front of the French teacher's house. They pass it almost hurriedly.

KOSMAS: And the shutters looking out on the road always closed.

NIKOS: I see you've checked things out.

KOSMAS: Whenever I came by here, they were always closed.

NIKOS: To hide the orgies going on inside.

25.

The shop is rather large. Piled up in the back are large wooden crates with cigarettes that have not yet been opened. To one side, shelves with a variety of novelties. A bald, bespectacled employee is getting an order ready. He crosses out every item he puts in the package from a list next to him. At the cashier's counter another elderly employee, also bald, Yiannis's uncle. He is checking some ledgers. Without raising his eyes from there he addresses himself to the other employee.

UNCLE: What did we do with that Mr. Kyriopoulos from Chrisovitsi?

PANTELIS: He said he sent a check.

Nikos and Kosmas walk into the store. The man at the cashier's desk looks at them. His expression is like that of a washed-out satyr.

NIKOS: Is Yiannis here?

UNCLE: He's out making a delivery. He won't be long.

Nikos turns toward Kosmas. At that moment Yiannis pulls up to the curb outside on his bicycle and brakes. He climbs off, steadies the bicycle against the curb of the sidewalk and pushes the door. On the door pane the sign forbidding military personnel from entering. He almost bumps into the other boys. He is pleasantly surprised.

YIANNIS: Hey, what's up?

He takes out two separate packets of money and gives them to the cashier.

YIANNIS: This is from Doulas. And that's from Kanakaris.

Then he turns toward Nikos and Kosmas.

YIANNIS: Two o'clock today, right?
NIKOS: Two o'clock this afternoon.

Yiannis walks toward the back. He leans against the crates of cigarettes. Nikos and Kosmas follow him.

KOSMAS: We came to take you out.

Yiannis addresses himself to the employee.

YIANNIS: Pantelis, are there any more orders?
PANTELIS: There are four ready to go.
YIANNIS: What then?
PANTELIS: There are still quite a few.
YIANNIS: (*to Kosmas*) Don't think I can join you.
NIKOS: What about your old man?
YIANNIS: They deported them. To Piraeus, and then CIF[11] to Icaria.
NIKOS: For a long time?
YIANNIS: Two or three months. As long as the operations are still being carried out.
KOSMAS: That's why the mountain combat units came here.

11. CIF is a maritime trade acronym for "Cost, Insurance and Freight," a contractual agreement denoting that overseas shipping expenses were paid by the sender. "Tsif," as the English initials were pronounced by Greeks, was a common acronym used in the late 1940s to imply the fast and direct dispatch of anyone and anything to its destination. Its use here to describe leftist prisoners being sent off to exile on the island of Icaria is ironic.

The uncle at the cash register interrupts them.

UNCLE: Yiannis, why don't you offer your friends a Turkish delight?

He takes a big box from a shelf behind him and puts it next to the cash register.

YIANNIS: My friends don't eat Turkish delights.

He winks at them and checks the bill of lading on a package that is ready to go.

YIANNIS: Is this for Mr. Kasiopoulos, Pantelis?
PANTELIS: Yes.
YIANNIS: Is there anything else in that neighborhood?
PANTELIS: The package I'm getting ready now.

The uncle takes an old Kodak box camera out of a drawer.

UNCLE: Well, then, let's take their picture.

He comes down from the cash register and walks toward them. He is short and limps on a dislocated hip.

YIANNIS: They don't want their picture taken either.

The uncle stops in front of them.

UNCLE: Not possible: Aren't you classmates? I'll take one picture of you as a memento, so you can remember your youth.

He has already put the camera to his eye and is focusing on them. Pantelis, tying the package on the other side of the room, smiles.

UNCLE: Ready.

The three strike a pose, smiling condescendingly. It is clear that they know the uncle and the tricks he is up to. The uncle deliberately takes a long time to create some suspense.

UNCLE: Ready . . . . . . Smile.

He presses the button. The front of the camera flips down and a huge rubber penis pops out. He is the first to laugh and without waiting for the reactions of the others he turns toward the cash register. Nikos and Kosmas applaud him.

YIANNIS: He's off his rocker.
NIKOS: He's just an old geezer, no?

Yiannis grabs the parcel from the counter and walks toward the exit.

KOSMAS: Can we help you?
YIANNIS: Take that one from Pantelis.

Nikos goes and opens the door for them. He addresses himself to the uncle.

NIKOS: When will we get the photographs?

The uncle pretends to be busy and smiles beneath his moustache.

UNCLE: They'll be ready tomorrow.

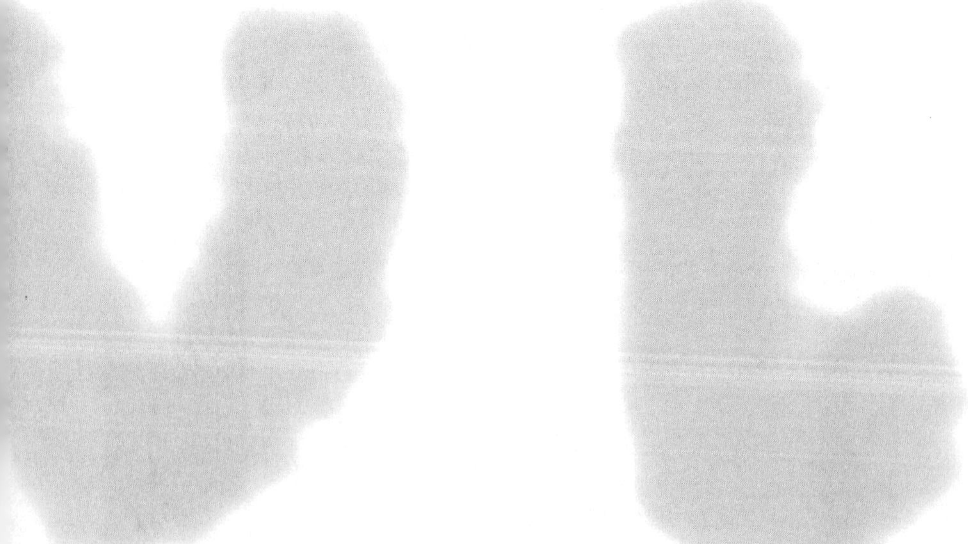

DAY FOUR

26.

A cement walkway cuts across the untended garden. The house at the back is one-floor, long and narrow. The last room has its own separate door. Continuing horizontally out from just past the room an add-on shack that serves as a common kitchen. Next to it, the bathroom.

Kosmas pushes the small door to the garden and goes inside. Nikos follows him. He stops short in the middle of the cement walkway, dumbstruck.

In front of the room, below the bare grapevine, hang freshly-washed sheets, a few towels, and some underwear. Nikos stops behind Kosmas.

NIKOS: What's all this?

Without answering Kosmas moves forward. Cautiously, he stands in front of his room and listens for a while. Then he takes hold of the doorknob, turns it noiselessly and pushes it inward. The door opens wide, revealing the inside of the room. It is rather large and above all it is tidy. In the center a brazier fully burning. The floor swept, the table with the few books dusted, the wide sofa beautifully decked out with new sheets and pillows. Kosmas turns and looks at Nikos standing startled next to him without speaking. From the direction of the kitchen hidden from view by the hanging sheets, the sound of a lid on a pot is heard. Kosmas carefully pushes the sheets aside, looking toward the sounds. The kitchen window is open. Inside a woman of thirty-five or forty with a spoon in her right hand, ready to taste the food. Sensing that they are watching her, she stops and slowly turns her head. She sees Kosmas. Her face lights up. She puts down the spoon and opens the door. She hugs Kosmas as he stands there in front of her and holds him close to her for a while. Kosmas pulls away and looks at her.

KOSMAS: When did you arrive?

MOTHER: You had just left. Your bed was still warm.

KOSMAS: Did you get the key from Madame Georgia?

MOTHER: Yes.

KOSMAS: Good thing you were in time to get it.

She is an attractive woman, she looks younger than her age.

KOSMAS: Why are you wearing black?

MOTHER: Your grandmother.

KOSMAS: She died?

MOTHER: (*She nods her head.*)

KOSMAS: When?

MOTHER: On Tuesday.

Kosmas remains silent. From behind the sheets Nikos appears.

KOSMAS: Mother, this is Nikos. My classmate from Alonistaina.

The mother smiles. They greet each other.

NIKOS: I should be going.

MOTHER: Why, Nikos?

Her voice is intimate and warm.

NIKOS: At two o'clock we have school.
MOTHER: Aren't you going together?
KOSMAS: Yes.
MOTHER: Then you'll stay. We'll have lunch together and then you'll both leave.

Nikos tries to get out of it.

NIKOS: You two must have things to talk about.
MOTHER: What we talk about is not a secret.

She doesn't give him time to react. She turns off the gas stove, takes a few plates from a cabinet and goes out toward the room.

MOTHER: Who will take the books off the table?

The two boys follow her.

MOTHER: Close the door. The room is freezing cold.

She gets them busy doing various minor chores. She places the plates on the table that they have cleared, and she gets a tablecloth from somewhere. She sends Kosmas to bring a chair from Madame Georgia's. She spreads out the tablecloth and asks Nikos, who has already fallen under her charms, to smooth it out better. She herself is in and out of the kitchen. Nikos is left by himself for a moment. With the feeling of the fresh tablecloth still on his hands. Across from him is the beautifully made-up large sofa.

ν πραμάτεια. Ο Β

τέρηση. Ακολουθε

τα. Ο πατέρας πε

, βιαστικός, με

DAY FIVE

27.

Kosmas and Nikos at the same desk. They have their French primers open in front of them but only as a pretext. From the classroom window the winter sky is visible. Nikos glances outside, then leans toward Kosmas. The teacher's voice reaches them faintly from her desk: they barely pay attention to her.

NIKOS: (*whispering*) Do you feel it?
KOSMAS: (*also whispering*) Feel what?
NIKOS: Put your hand here.

He places his palm on the bench where they are seated. Kosmas does the same.

NIKOS: Nothing?
KOSMAS: No.

Nikos shakes his head bitterly.

NIKOS: The heat.

After a short while.

NIKOS: Can't you feel it passing from the wood to your thighs and fanning up toward your kidneys?

Kosmas smiles.

NIKOS: (*poetically*) The heat from their beautiful bodies.

Suddenly he changes tone.

NIKOS: Who could have been sitting here?

Kosmas shrugs his shoulders.

NIKOS: (*inspired*) Do you know something? Give me your pen.

KOSMAS: What do you want it for?

NIKOS: I'm going to write a message.

KOSMAS: To whom?

NIKOS: To her.

KOSMAS: What will you write?

NIKOS: (*puzzled*) What should I write?

KOSMAS: "You are the object of my dreams."

NIKOS: Excellent. Give me your pen.

Kosmas gives it to him.

KOSMAS: Be careful not to scratch the nib against the wood.

Nikos reassures him. He begins to write. *"To my unknown beauty: You are the object of my dreams."* He stands for a while looking aslant at it to see if the letters are legible.

NIKOS: Can you see them?

KOSMAS: From here, yes.

The sound of a ruler tapping on the teacher's desk. They are startled. They turn their attention toward the sound. The teacher steps up to the blackboard. She explains certain grammatical rules to them. Suddenly someone in the front stands up and turns toward the back silently waving a pair of girls' panties he found on the shelf under his desk. In a flash and before the first stifled laughs erupt, he sits back down in his place as though nothing at all has happened. The teacher turns toward the class. With a stern expression.

FRENCH TEACHER: What is going on?

She looks at them slowly, her gaze sweeping over them. The class plays dumb.

FRENCH TEACHER: Next time I will examine you on all this. And I will accept no excuses.

She glances at her watch. The bell rings for the break. The teacher collects her papers and stiffly exits. There is an immediate commotion behind her. The same student with the panties has climbed on a desk and is waving them like a trophy. Someone tries to snatch them from him. At the last minute he flings them toward the other end of the room. A wild game is now underway on the desks with shouting and the girls' panties tossed from hand to hand. A windowpane breaks. Then the principal appears in the doorway. Behind him teachers roused by the uproar. Before he even realizes what is happening, the principal feels a piece of cloth hit him in the face. He catches it just in time before it falls to the floor. The rowdy boys freeze. Surprised amidst their silence the principal realizes what he is holding in his hands. With some embarrassment he turns and shows it to the others behind him.

28.

The lowering of the flag. Sunset. The last frigid rays of sun are poised on the top of the marble bell tower of the Cathedral. In the square a few idle passersby. In its center on a tall metal pole the flag is waving. A platoon falls in line for the lowering of the flag. The trumpet calls everyone to attention. People stop moving. The officer in charge gives the appropriate commands, the section presents arms. A corporal slowly lowers the flag to the familiar sound of the trumpet, folds it, and returns to his place. The section now exits in the midst of the people who have once again begun to move about.

29.

A sweet shop. The waiter with a tray filled with pastries and glasses of water. He sets it down on one of the tables. At another table Kosmas, his mother, and Nikos. Nikos signals the waiter so he can pay him. The mother tries to talk him out of it.

NIKOS: No. The pastries are my treat. And Kosmas and I will buy the tickets for the theater.

He pays the waiter and gets his change.

KOSMAS: We've set our minds on giving you a good time and you can't refuse us.

The mother laughs. The boys' good intentions flatter her.

MOTHER: As for the pastries, OK, I thank you. I thank Nikos. But I won't come to the theater. If you want, the two of you can go.

KOSMAS: Why, mother?

MOTHER: Because I'm in mourning, Kosmas. It isn't proper.

KOSMAS: But no one is going to see you, we don't know anyone here.

MOTHER: The problem is not whether someone sees me or not. You two can go.

NIKOS: No, we won't go either.

He gets up first. The others follow, At the door he steps aside so the mother can exit first. It has begun to get dark out. The street lights have been turned on. Although it is cold, there is some activity by people seeking female company. Small groups of friends are out braving the cold weather. For a while they walk along the central street. A group of three girls comes toward them from across the way. The three are arm in arm. They pass by the boys. After a short while Nikos discreetly turns his head back. He catches them doing the same. They arrive outside the small gate to the garden. Nikos comes to a momentary halt.

MOTHER: Why don't you come in?
NIKOS: No. Good night. I'm going to study.
KOSMAS: Like hell you are!
MOTHER: I'll roast you some chestnuts on the brazier.

Nikos laughs.

NIKOS: No thanks.
MOTHER: Well then, good night.
NIKOS: Are you leaving tomorrow?
MOTHER: Yes, Nikos, I'm leaving tomorrow.

Nikos pulls up his coat collar and takes a few steps backward.

NIKOS: Good night.
MOTHER: Good night, Nikos.

They push the gate and walk along the small cement walkway. Just before they disappear beneath the shadow of the house and under the grapevine, the mother takes Kosmas's arm, hangs onto him tightly, and they start slowly running.

Nikos, enveloped by the darkness, can no longer make them out. He hears the door open and suddenly its square shape is lit up. It is closed immediately. Nikos remains in place for a while. Then he turns and begins to slowly move away, in silence.

ουν. Οι
οσμάς λα-
ι του πα-
νηντόρης,
μεγάλα σί-

DAY SIX

30.

Courtyard of the Girls High School. Morning. The boys' classes assembled. Someone recites the morning prayer. There is a light invisible rainfall. The prayer comes to an end, but the assembled classes continue to remain in their place. Mihalis turns and looks at Kosmas quizzically. A teacher comes out from inside with a large clothbound book. He gives it to the principal. The principal gestures for him to go ahead by himself. The teacher opens the book and begins to read.

TEACHER: In view of the fact that it was not possible to identify those responsible for the improprieties recently observed at the 7th Classical Lyceum during and immediately following the French class on 22.1.1948, and because the responsibility for the disturbance belongs to the entire class, the following students, drawn by lot, are given as punishment a three-day suspension:

Apostolopoulos, Athanasios
Zaharakos, Ilias
Kitsiopoulos, Evangelos
Granias, Nikolaos
Tzanis, Ioannis

This makes an impression on the boys. Nikos is startled hearing his name. The gym teachers blow their whistles. The classes begin to file one by one into the classrooms. Kosmas turns toward Nikos.

KOSMAS: What are you going to do?
NIKOS: What do you want me to do?

KOSMAS: Will you stay here or go back to the village?

NIKOS: I'm not going to the village. Why don't you go to yours?

He says this aggressively. Kosmas is taken aback. He has no time to answer. The class begins to move inside.

31.

Nikos's room is open. The hallway with the windowpanes deserted, illuminated by a weak noontime sun. From the direction of the kitchen the sound of a burning gas stove filters out. The bell of the entrance door rings. Nikos steps out of his room with a checkered kitchen towel in his hand. He goes to the side of the stairs and presses the button. The door opens, pushed from the outside. Kosmas appears. Nikos turns round and goes into the kitchen. On the burning gas stove a frying pan with half-cooked potatoes. Nikos throws the towel over his shoulders and stirs the potatoes with a fork. Kosmas's footsteps on the stairs. Then in the hallway. He walks into the kitchen.

KOSMAS: Hi.
NIKOS: Hi.

They are quiet. Nikos continues stirring the potatoes. Eventually he stops. He turns and looks at Kosmas.

NIKOS: Sorry about this morning.
KOSMAS: Sometimes I just don't understand you.
NIKOS: I don't either.

He turns off the gas stove and empties the potatoes onto a plate.

NIKOS: Have you eaten?
KOSMAS: Yes.

Nikos tosses the frying pan into the sink and turns on the water for a minute. He takes the plate and goes into his room. Kosmas follows him. Nikos puts the plate on the table with his books. He has cleared a small space there. On another towel laid out there is a piece of cheese and two or three water-soaked pieces of hardtack. And a pitcher of water. He pulls up a chair and sits down. Kosmas is now standing at the window looking outside.

NIKOS: Why don't you sit down?

Kosmas comes and stands over him, takes a potato and tastes it.

NIKOS: What happened at school?

KOSMAS: Nothing.

NIKOS: Did Lampsanas do his class?

KOSMAS: He didn't show up, he was chosen for jury duty.

NIKOS: Did anyone say anything about the suspensions?

KOSMAS: Vogaris did.

Nikos looks at him.

KOSMAS: Stefanou picked a fight with him. He told him that that kind of punishment is quite clearly arbitrary.

Nikos begins to show some interest.

NIKOS: And what did Vogaris say?

KOSMAS: That all punishments are arbitrary anyway.

NIKOS: He always slips away like an eel.

KOSMAS: Yes, because when you make an argument to go him one better, he suddenly takes things even further.

KOSMAS: And of course he was his usual humorous self.

NIKOS: What do you mean?

KOSMAS: He describes our reactions as barbaric. In view of such a poetic object.

NIKOS: Did he really say that?

KOSMAS: Exactly that. "A poetic object."

NIKOS: (*smiling*) That son-of-a-bitch.

Kosmas takes another potato and goes and sits on Nikos's bed. Nikos fills his glass with water. As he drinks it, Kosmos addresses him:

KOSMAS: You have a letter to write.

Still drinking, Nikos turns and looks at Kosmas. He empties the glass and rests it on the table and silently looks at Kosmas again.

KOSMAS: The unknown beauty replied.

NIKOS: What?

He jumps up full of enthusiasm.

NIKOS: Tell me what happened?

Kosmas smiles.

NIKOS: Tell me.

KOSMAS: Dreams.

Nikos gets angry.

NIKOS: What does that mean?

KOSMAS: That was her response: "Dreams." With an explanation point and five periods.

Nikos is disappointed.

KOSMAS: Not enough for you, eh?

NIKOS: I think it's ambiguous.

He clears the table, pushing the crumbs into his plate and goes and leaves it in the kitchen. Kosmas follows him.

KOSMAS: She's giving you an opening.

NIKOS: Yeah, but she may be putting us on.

He tosses the plate in the sink and goes back into the room.

KOSMAS: At any rate, if you approve after the fact, I took the liberty of answering for you,

Nikos turns and looks at him.

NIKOS: What do you mean?

KOSMAS: I wrote that she should be expecting a letter tomorrow.

NIKOS: Where?

KOSMAS: Behind the toilet tank.

Nikos laughs. He goes into his room. Kosmas follows him. He closes the door behind him.

KOSMAS: why are you laughing?

NIKOS: Imagine if Vogaris finds out about this. A love-letter in a toilet booth.

Kosmas goes back and sits on the bed again, he lies partially back, supporting himself on his elbows. Nikos stands for a while with his back to the window. He has suddenly grown serious.

NIKOS: Do you think we should write something, huh?

KOSMAS: Yes.

NIKOS: And what would someone write?

KOSMAS: We'll figure something out. Sit down and get a pencil.

Nikos sits down at the table. Kosmas gazes outside toward the sunlight

KOSMAS: My beautiful unknown damsel . . .

NIKOS: Isn't that a bit hackneyed nowadays?

Kosmas does not reply. He seems to be lost in reverie. In the distance a woman's voice can be heard calling a child.

Annie . . . Annie . . .

At that moment Kosmas turns back toward Nikos.

KOSMAS: Guess what? Tonight is the first night of the new moon. . . .

32.

Darkness. Someone is moving along the stone wall of the French teacher's house. He stops and looks around him carefully. Then he looks at the height of the fence as though measuring it. Behind the treetops the narrow new crescent moon shines brightly. Kosmas leaps then and there onto a saddle-like hump in the stone wall, he straddles it and jumps into the garden. He lands softly and remains motionless for a while trying to orient himself. In the back the lights from the windows of the house shine on the tree trunks in front of them. Bending low he walks cautiously toward them. He stops behind a bush. A few meters in front of him the French teacher's room with the lights on. Through the wide one-piece window one can see the entire inside space. A stove is burning in the middle. On the walls are shelves with books. Also a large spacious desk laden with a good number of books. Across from there on the other side is a well-made bed. The French teacher herself sitting comfortably in a bamboo armchair with a book. She has stopped reading, she remains motionless for some time, lost in thought. From a teapot on the small table next to her she refills her teacup, throws in some sugar, slowly stirs it in and just as slowly takes a sip. She puts down the book, gets up, and disappears in the inner recesses of the house. She returns with a glass of water and a nightgown that she spreads on an armchair next to the stove. Standing, she begins to brush her hair mechanically, while at the same time she has another sip of tea, sets a small alarm clock, and fills the stove with wood. She goes back out and returns immediately without the hairbrush and closes the door behind her. She turns on the lamp next to the bed and turns off the overhead lights. The room is now bathed in a soft low light. She stands motionless for a while looking around her, then takes off her robe, and as she is half-hidden by the stovepipes she removes her underwear — first her bra, then her panties — she puts on her nightgown, walks toward the bed and, leaning over, turns off the lamp. The room is plunged in darkness.

DAY SEVEN

33.

A shoemaker's. Kosmas is seated on an old-looking sofa covered with worn oilcloth. He has already put on one boot and is trying to put on the other. The shop owner, stooping in front of him, helps him. Kosmas ties the laces and stands up.

SHOP OWNER: How do they fit?

Kosmas takes a few steps, stops, takes a few more steps.

SHOP OWNER: They're a little tight, eh?
KOSMAS: Yes.
SHOP OWNER: It's nothing. If you wear them once or twice they'll stretch. Will you take them off or should I wrap up the old ones?
KOSMAS: I'll take them off.
He sits on the sofa, he takes them off, he puts on his old boots. The shop owner takes the new ones, wraps them up carefully in some newspaper and ties them. Kosmas leaves the rest of his money on the counter.

SHOP OWNER: Wear them in good health.
KOSMAS: Thank you.

34.

Light rain. Kosmas walks for a while along the sidewalk. The rainfall grows stronger and he is forced to stop under a metal awning. For a while he watches the rain pensively. Mihalis appears from around the corner across the street. He is holding an open black umbrella. One of its ribs is broken. He stops across from Kosmas.

KOSMAS: Where are you off to?
MIHALIS: To the library.

Mihalis is about to step down into the street. A jeep with Military Police drives by between them splashing up muddy water. Mihalis jumps back and watches it speed away. Then he crosses the street and goes over to Kosmas.

MIHALIS: And what are you doing?
KOSMAS: I'm looking for Nikos.
MIHALIS: Isn't he at home?
KOSMAS: No.

They are blocking the sidewalk and someone apologetically asks permission to pass.

35.

The interior of a book and stationery store. In the rear the cashier. A female employee on a ladder is stretching to get something from the highest shelves. Kosmas and Mihalis come in. They are eying the girl's partially revealed hips, but it seems they have been caught in the act by another employee behind the opposite counter who is looking at them inquisitively. They move toward him. Mihalis takes an old American pen from the inside pocket of his jacket.

MIHALIS: The ink sac is broken on this one. Can we change it?

The employee silently takes the pen and skillfully unscrews it. While he is doing this Kosmas turns his head cautiously back. The girl has climbed down from the ladder and is carrying it to the rear. At the same time Vogaris comes in through the entrance door. He says a general sort of hello and walks toward Mihalis and Kosmas. The employee looks up smiling.

EMPLOYEE: Your order is ready.

He turns and shouts toward the back of the shop.

EMPLOYEE: Stavroula . . .
GREEK LIT. TEACHER: Please finish with the boys first.
EMPLOYEE: But we're done with the boys.

He has already replaced the ink sac and put the pen back together. The saleswoman comes over to him.

EMPLOYEE: Bring the teacher's book.

She opens an inkwell and fills the pen with ink. She tests it on a large pad next to it and gives it to Mihalis for him to try out too.

MIHALIS: What do I owe you?
EMPLOYEE: Go pay at the cashier.
GREEK LIT. TEACHER: Beautiful old Parker pen.
MIHALIS: A gift from America, Sir.

The girl brings a book and rests it on the counter.

EMPLOYEE: Shall I wrap it?

The Greek Literature teacher is already holding it and leafing through it.

GREEK LIT. TEACHER: No need to.

He goes over to the cashier and pays. Mihalis has also paid. Kosmas is waiting at the exit door. They let the Greek Literature teacher go out first.

The rain, which had let up, somehow begins to come down again. Mihalis tries his umbrella. He half-opens it, then he closes it. They stand under the metal awning.

MIHALIS: Do you want us to take you somewhere, Sir?
GREEK LIT. TEACHER: Do you think three of us could fit under the same umbrella?

Mihalis laughs.

MIHALIS: I'm afraid not.

KOSMAS: And a defective umbrella at that.

MIHALIS: Not at all defective. It's just missing a rib.

GREEK LIT. TEACHER: At any rate, thank you for the offer. And where are you boys going?

MIHALIS: To the library.

GREEK LIT. TEACHER: Time to study. Time for study and for contemplation. Time to be indoors.

KOSMAS: What about you, Sir?

His glance falls on the book the Greek literature teacher is holding.

GREEK LIT. TEACHER: Do you mean what I'm reading or what I'm going to read?

He gives him the book. Kosmas examines it.

GREEK LIT. TEACHER: It's a book whose heroes are your age, or rather they're not. They're younger. But I don't know if it's a book for boys your age.

KOSMAS: Why do you say that?

GREEK LIT. TEACHER: Because some things we only discover when we are well past them. Like, shall we say, an awareness about adolescence . . .

He changes tone as though he no longer wants to elaborate on this.

GREEK LIT. TEACHER: But it's a beautiful, tender book.

Kosmas gives it back to him.

KOSMAS: Even though you haven't read it yet.

The Greek literature teacher laughs.

GREEK LIT. TEACHER: Yes, you're right.

It's as though he is injecting a pause into the conversation. He buttons his coat and gets ready to leave.

GREEK LIT. TEACHER: The rain has let up. Well then, as soon as I finish the book, I will let you know my definitive opinion.

He waves goodbye to them and leaves. They watch him for a while as he disappears under the arcades.

36.

Mihalis and Kosmas are crossing the narrow stone-paved walkway; they turn at the corner of the building and begin to climb the outer stone stairs to the library. High on the large, covered balcony a frail old man with a short-trimmed gray beard, Vangelis and another of their classmates, Alekos. Vangelis turns toward them in a state of euphoria.

VANGELIS: You missed it . . . The "general" recited "The Orange Girl."[12] With extraordinary verve and inspiration.

The "general," pleased with himself, flicks the ashes from his cigarette; his eyes are shining.

GENERAL: The verve is transmitted by the poem itself; it's inherent in it. I merely recited it!

MIHALIS: The "Orange Girl."

ALEKOS: To the "general's" orange girl, who is studiously and devotedly poring over a cheap romance novel in the library reading room.

GENERAL: Come now, gentlemen, no personal allusions.

From the balcony the rooftops of part of the city are visible; a marble bell tower half hidden by the light rain, and behind it the tops of tall pine trees.

12. "The Orange Girl," or "Portokalenia" in its original Greek, is a poem by Odysseus Elytis — Nobel Prize Winner, 1979 — in which a sun-intoxicated female beauty metamorphoses, by slow degrees, and to cosmic exaltations, into the "little Orange Girl." The poem first appeared in Elytis's 1943 collection *Ilios o protos (Sun: The Primordial),* while Greece was still under German occupation.

37.

Kosmas leaves them there teasing the "general," he pushes the entrance door and goes inside. Behind the glass panes in the lobby the entire reading room of the library is visible. Nikos, at one of the tables with a book open in front of him, is leaning over writing. At another table two girls, one a strawberry blonde, clearly the "general's" Orange Girl. Kosmas walks cautiously toward Nikos. Nikos realizes it's him at the last minute. Kosmas, holding one of the small forms one has to fill out to take out books, sits down beside him. In addition to the two girls there are a few more readers scattered around the reading room. In the rear, at her own small desk, the aging librarian. A tall woman, harsh, and somewhat hunched over. In a whisper, so as not to disturb anyone, Kosmas addresses himself to Nikos.

KOSMAS: Why didn't you say you were coming here?

NIKOS: I was going to stop by your place later.

Kosmas takes the open book from in front of Nikos and examines it. *The Charterhouse of Parma.* Nikos collects his various papers.

KOSMAS: Is it her you're writing to?

NIKOS: Yes.

KOSMAS: Why don't you press her to answer your proposal?

NIKOS: She answered.

KOSMAS: (*surprised*) When?

NIKOS: Today.

KOSMAS: (*upset*) Why didn't you say anything?

In the rear the librarian, looking reproachfully in their direction, lightly taps a small ruler on the desk, compelling them to be silent. At that moment Vangelis and the others walk into the lobby. The break is over, the "general" has tossed away his cigarette. While Mihalis attempts to fit his umbrella into a brass container, the others tiptoe forward toward their seats. Nikos, determined to leave, collects his things. He sees the package Kosmas has left in front of him.

NIKOS: What have you got there?
KOSMAS: I got my shoes.

Nikos gets to his feet.

NIKOS: Let's go.

He walks over and turns in his book. Kosmas follows him. In the hallway toward the exit they bump into Mihalis.

MIHALIS: (*whispering*) Are you leaving?
NIKOS: Yes.

They step into the lobby and just before they leave, Kosmas glances behind him. He sees the two girls looking in their direction smiling.

38.

They step out onto the balcony, Nikos first, Kosmas behind him. Nikos takes out a letter and gives it to him.

NIKOS: Read it.

His tone is imperious; this is his response to Kosmas's teasing.

Kosmas takes the letter, puts his shoes under his arm, reads a few lines, silently looks at Nikos and walks down a few more stairs. He stops again and begins reading aloud.

KOSMAS: *Dearest, dearest . . .*

His tone of voice is somewhat exaggerated. He stops one more time and addresses himself to Nikos.

KOSMAS: What would Vogaris call that, "a repetitive construction"?
NIKOS: Why are you making fun of me?
KOSMAS: (*ambiguously*) Out of jealousy.

He climbs down the remaining stairs. Nikos behind him. The rain has stopped, but the atmosphere continues to be damp and cloudy. Walking slowly along the stone-paved walkway, Kosmas continues reading. His tone similarly exaggerated as before, perhaps to provoke Nikos. Bit by bit, however, what he reads completely captures his attention.

KOSMAS: *Your persistence has won me over. How can I counter the fire in what you write me. What powers can I summon to resist the deluge of your feelings? How can I tame the tempests they have roused in me?*

Kosmas now serious turns and looks at Nikos in a more critical frame of mind after everything that has now been revealed about how Nikos himself handled his correspondence. Nikos, silent, closes himself off defensively.

KOSMAS: *Dearest, dearest. I will not reveal my name to you, as you ask, I will reveal my innermost self. On Sunday at three in the afternoon, whatever the weather, we will be walking along the route from Taxiarhes to Aigli to Ayiou Georgiou. I will be with my friend Dorothea Lefkou. Do you know her? Answer and tell me who you will be with. But even if you are not with anyone, I will recognize you. My impatient heart will recognize you, it will know you, dearest.*

Kosmas stops at the metal gate leading to the street. He is impressed by the way this story is playing itself out. Nikos has also stopped. They remain silent for a while.

KOSMAS: What did you answer her.
NIKOS: That I'd be with you.
KOSMAS: "With my friend Dorothea Lefkou." Who on earth does this person hang out with? Do you think it's Georgiadou?

Nikos does not answer. Kosmas is beside himself.

KOSMAS: It must be her. Wow . . .

Suddenly, as excitedly as he began, Kosmas stops. Nikos's silence, his reserve, spills over to Kosmas too. They go out onto the street. They get as far as another small square with a circular garden in the middle and bare weeping willows. An old man with high rubber galoshes and a folded sack on his head to protect himself from the rain has already stopped and is watering the soggy garden with a hose. In the background, behind the sparse gray clouds in the gray sky there is a slight hint of sunset. They stop and silently take in this bizarre scene. The old man continues his watering indifferently. At a certain moment Kosmas turns to Nikos.

KOSMAS: Do you know what?

Nikos stares at him silently.

KOSMAS: The French teacher spends her nights alone.

DAY EIGHT

39.

Nikos's room. Nikos pulls out his pants from under the mattress. He has put them there to be pressed. He inspects them and sets them on a chair. Standing on the table is a small mirror. Using his finger and a bit of soapy water Nikos wets the pronounced dark fuzz over his upper lip and shaves it. Then he shaves his two cheeks in the same way. He wipes himself with a towel and remains for some time staring at his face in the mirror. On his right sideburn and slightly below some invisible cut a small drop of blood is forming. Nikos watches it enraptured as it takes shape and suddenly breaks free and trickles down his cheek.

40.

Late Sunday afternoon in the large vacant lot. Bright, sunny day. Kosmas supporting himself on his bicycle watches Nikos repeat his risky attempts to race up onto the embankment that leads to the cement water pipe. He doesn't make it and in the end he turns and speeds toward Kosmas. He brakes suddenly next to him, his tires dragging through the mud.

KOSMAS: Hey, man, are you hell-bent on killing yourself today?

Nikos smiles silently. His face is somewhat sweaty. The cathedral clock chimes audibly in the distance. Three o'clock. Nikos looks Kosmas in the eye. As though he were trying to get his own agitation under control.

NIKOS: Shall we get going?

They begin walking on foot, slowly pushing their bicycles. Kosmas is wearing his new shoes. They go into the street. Silent. Nikos stops.

NIKOS: Do you know what?
KOSMAS: No.

Nikos gets angry.

NIKOS: So tell me, did you come along to give me support or make nasty comments?

KOSMAS: Take it easy, man. You asked me do I know what and I said no. Is that making a comment?

Nikos ignores Kosmas's mocking tone. He sobers up and wipes his slightly sweaty palms on his pants.

NIKOS: Maybe it would be better if we didn't show up right away.

KOSMAS: What do you mean?

NIKOS: Mmm, we could stop somewhere. Behind the trees.

KOSMAS: Why?

NIKOS: We'll let them pass us by and then jump on our bikes and catch up with them.

KOSMAS: Do you think that's fair?

NIKOS: Why are you bringing up fairness?

KOSMAS: So tell me, are you nervous?

NIKOS: No.

KOSMAS: Well, I am.

NIKOS: A good reason to help me out.

KOSMAS: Let's stop and wait for them. But suppose they don't show up?

NIKOS: If they don't show up we'll leave.

They get off the street and walk partially up toward a field and disappear among the pine trees bordering it.

41.

The sound of the Cathedral clock chiming the half hour can be heard. Kosmas and Nikos have left their bicycles on a ridge behind them and watch the road hidden in some bushes. At a certain moment Kosmas shoves Nikos. Nikos looks in the direction Kosmas is showing him. Far off at the top of the crest of the road two girls gradually come into view. The initial burst of excitement is followed by an impassive state which will soon turn into complete disappointment, especially for Nikos, when they understand without a doubt that the girls are truly the ones they are waiting for. Next to the lovely Dorothea walks a homely fat girl with glasses. As they approach the place where the boys are, Kosmas whispers to Nikos.

KOSMAS: Who is that?

Nikos doesn't answer. He is frozen in place. As the girls pass by unaware of them, Nikos gets up, gets on his bicycle without speaking and takes off. Kosmas turns toward him, but cannot even raise his voice to shout.

KOSMAS: Where are you going?

Nikos has already disappeared at the other end of the trees. Kosmas gets up, gets on his bicycle in turn and pedals off after him.

42.

Kosmas on the road to the vacant lot. Far ahead of him he sees Nikos disappear down the hill. He increases his speed and when he reaches the hill out of breath, he stops cold in his tracks: Nikos has finally managed to get up on the embankment and, balancing himself like an acrobat, is crossing, still on his bike, the suspended cement water pipe. Kosmas stifles his first impulse to shout, and holding his breath watches Nikos come out at the other end. Then he screams out his name.

KOSMAS: Nikos . . .

Not only does Nikos not answer, he does not even stop to look behind him. Jamming madly down on the pedals he disappears in the fields surrounding the vacant lot.

υπάλληλ

χαν ιασμ

τέρα το

DAY NINE

43.

School is out. Children pour out onto the street. Next to the gate is a four-wheel stand with nuts, candies, etc. From a small funnel in its center a thin stream of smoke is rising. Mihalis walks over to the stand and buys something. Kosmas waits for him a little further away. Another student comes over to Kosmas.

STUDENT: What happened to Granias? Is he out sick?

KOSMAS: I don't think so.

STUDENT: Will you be seeing him?

KOSMAS: Yes.

STUDENT: I lent him my algebra notes and I need them back now.

KOSMAS: I'll tell him.

Mihalis comes over with a paper cone filled with peanuts. He offers Kosmas some and the two walk along the sidewalk.

MIHALIS: Why did Nikos run out on us again?

Kosmas shrugs his shoulders without answering. They walk together as far as the next corner. Mihalis leaves. At the entrance to the hotel across from them a colonel is saying good-bye to a young woman. She is pretty, well dressed, she looks like someone from Athens. He bends and kisses her hand. The second lieutenant accompanying her, an intellectual-looking type with glasses and his revolver lanyard looped around his neck, salutes the colonel. The colonel salutes him back and gets into the jeep waiting for him further along. The couple goes into the hotel. Kosmas, who has stopped to take in this scene, continues on his way.

44.

Early afternoon. In the courtyard of a church some boys are playing a half-field soccer game. The ball scoots away at a certain point and Nikos, who is watching the game, jumps up, stops it skillfully and sends it back. Then he sees Kosmas on his right, next to the railing at the entrance. He has been standing there watching Nikos. For how long? Nikos hesitates a bit, but in the end walks over toward Kosmas.

NIKOS: How did you find me?

KOSMAS: I rang the bell at your house and then I heard the shouting.

He continues to stand outside the metal gate.

KOSMAS: You're making good use of your time, I see.

NIKOS: Is that what you came here to tell me?

KOSMAS: Not exactly.

NIKOS: Why don't you come inside?

KOSMAS: Not inside. If you like, let's go for a walk.

NIKOS: Where?

KOSMAS: Anywhere at all.

Nikos is hesitant.

KOSMAS: Peppas wants his algebra notes, the ones he lent you.

NIKOS: Yeah, dammit, I forgot them. Shall we go to my house and I'll give them to you?

KOSMAS: Why should you give them to me? What am I, the errand boy here?

NIKOS: Sorry, I didn't mean it that way.

KOSMAS: Listen, I don't want to get into a quarrel with you. If you're in a bad mood I'd rather just leave.

He turns and walks off a way.

NIKOS: Kosmas . . .

Kosmas stops. Nikos goes up to him.

KOSMAS: What's going on with you? Yesterday you didn't come to school at all, OK? Same thing today. And if I'm reading things right you won't come tomorrow either.

NIKOS: I can't, Kosmas.

KOSMAS: What's the matter with you?

NIKOS: Please don't talk to me like that. At least not in that tone of voice.

Kosmas looks at him for a while, then begins to walk slowly, pulling Nikos half-willingly along with him.

KOSMAS: OK, so you can't. What next?

NIKOS: I can't sit at the same desk. I feel ridiculous. With all that heat from their lovely bodies. Shit.

KOSMAS: So let's say that's how things are. How are you going to deal with it? By burying your head in the sand?

NIKOS: I don't know.

KOSMAS: Can I ask you something?

Nikos comes to a halt.

KOSMAS: Do you feel ridiculous or exposed?

NIKOS: Exposed to whom?

KOSMAS: To yourself.

Nikos is speechless.

Three houses further along a door opens. It is a few steps up from the street. A pretty young woman is making her way down to the sidewalk. She converses briefly with someone inside and moves away. Kosmas and Nikos have stopped walking. The woman comes up near them. Behind her the head of a middle-aged man peers out of the open door. He is wearing pajamas and a bathrobe over them. He sees the boys, watches the woman moving steadily away, and disappears inside again. The woman passes the boys. Kosmas and Nikos continue on their way. For some time the woman's high-heeled shoes can be heard behind them on the cement squares of the sidewalk as she moves away.

NIKOS: Maybe you're right. It was all really just some kind of cowardice, wasn't it? To inspect the goods out of sight and then to scoot off like a hare.

KOSMAS: Wouldn't anyone have done the same?

NIKOS: I don't know. Maybe.

KOSMAS: Or would you prefer not to have hidden?

Nikos doesn't answer.

KOSMAS: And I missed out on that pretty thing. I lost my chance to get something going with her. Dorothea. I mean, Dorothea. But even if we'd met up with them. Wouldn't that have been worse for you?

NIKOS: It depends.

Kosmas is surprised.

KOSMAS: What do you mean?

Nikos doesn't answer.

KOSMAS: You're driving me crazy. What's the problem? That you hid and then scooted off or that you didn't meet the young lady herself?

NIKOS: The problem is that I know.

Nikos's incisive response surprises Kosmas. Instead of continuing, Nikos takes two loose cigarettes from his pocket.

NIKOS: Want one?

Kosmas refuses. He makes no comment about the fact that Nikos has begun to smoke. Nikos inhales once or twice — still a bit awkwardly.

NIKOS: She doesn't know a thing, she doesn't know who wrote her the impassioned words. OK, it's no big deal. But I wrote that and I know I did. And I believed it, do you understand? And all of a sudden I don't believe it. Because she wears glasses? Because she's fat? And if she wasn't fat and didn't wear glasses?

They are now walking down the main street. Nikos tosses his cigarette away, angry at himself and lost in thought.

Kosmas tries to say something.

KOSMAS: Now listen . . .

But he doesn't go on. And Nikos seems to be somewhere else. From the speakers of the "Avra" movie theater the song "Amapola"[13] is playing. Although it is still daytime, the entrance lights to the theater are all on. They stop in front of the promotional photographs for the movie *Blood and Sand.* Tyrone Power — Rita Hayworth. People are looking at a photograph of Hayworth.

KOSMAS: Now, imagine what I could write about her.

His effort to somehow lighten the atmosphere does not work. His pleasantry is wasted. Nikos has already moved a few steps forward. Kosmas catches up to him and they continue on together. Kosmas limps imperceptibly in his uncomfortable new shoes.

13. The Spanish American composer and lyricist Joseph Lacalle authored the international hit "Amapola" in 1920. The well-known love song became popular in Greece in "Danae" Stratigopoulou's interpretation in 1933.

45.

Sunset. The light in the park is strange, almost unreal. Nikos, slightly ahead, stops every now and then, says something or nothing at all, and then, as though he cannot calm down, he starts in again. Their walk is filled with visual surprises. Sometimes they come upon a clear blue sky, and other times an opening in the trees like a tunnel that leads nowhere.

NIKOS: I'm disgusted and angry at myself. And I'm ashamed. I'm ashamed, you don't know how ashamed I am. Maybe you're right. Maybe it's just my wounded ego. Ridiculous and exposed. Why can't you just take a sponge and erase it all . . .

KOSMAS: But you can forget it.

Nikos doesn't answer. They have come to a small hill. On their right a row of cypress trees extends, closing off the western side of the park. They stand there silently and watch the sun sink behind lead grey clouds.

DAY TEN

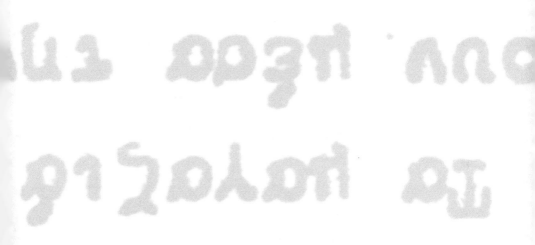

46.

Break. Distribution of morning snack.

47.

A taxi stops outside the high school. A middle-aged man gets out wearing army boots and an ascot around his scrawny neck. The driver opens the trunk, he takes out a heavy carton and places it on the sidewalk. The middle-aged man pays him, the taxi leaves. He remains alone staring for a moment at the empty school yard. Then he takes out a handkerchief and meticulously wipes the dust first from one then from his other boot. He glances at the yard again and lifting the carton with both hands goes inside and walks toward the offices.

48.

A classroom. Mr. Vogaris at the front desk. He is giving the boys the schedule for the first semester exams.

The door suddenly opens and the woman in charge of maintenance enters almost noiselessly. She approaches the front desk, says something to the teacher and goes back out. The boys' curiosity is temporarily aroused. Vogaris glances at them for a minute and continues.

GREEK LIT. TEACHER: So, is everything clear? Are there any questions?

Someone raises his hand.

GREEK LIT. TEACHER: Yes?

The student gets up from his desk.

STUDENT: About the history exam, Sir . . .

GREEK LIT. TEACHER: Yes.

STUDENT: Will we be examined on all of our coursework?

GREEK LIT. TEACHER: What do you mean?

STUDENT: Just that. Will we be examined on all of the coursework?

GREEK LIT. TEACHER: Why, what else could you be asked about, I mean.

The student becomes slightly unnerved. Various snickers and comments can be heard.

GREEK LIT. TEACHER: Quiet. Of course you will be examined on all the coursework. Anyone else? Are there any more questions?

He looks at the class with a sweeping glance.

GREEK LIT. TEACHER: Danakas? Granias?
NIKOS: No, Sir . . .
GREEK LIT. TEACHER: Then we're finished for today.

Some students jump up immediately, ready to leave.

GREEK LIT. TEACHER: Wait a minute. You may go out, but no one may leave. An order from the principal.

The boys' curiosity is aroused again. The teacher gathers up his papers and exits without speaking.

49.

The principal in his office. In the corner the man with the boots and the ascot. There is a knock on the door.

PRINCIPAL: Come in.

Vogaris enters.

GREEK LIT. TEACHER: You asked to see me?

PRINCIPAL: This is from the Military Administration of the Peloponnese.

He holds out a typed document to him, stamped and signed, motioning him to sit at the same time.

PRINCIPAL: They recommend that we allow this gentleman, Mister . . .

GENTLEMAN: Trikorfiotis.

PRINCIPAL: . . . to recite his poems to the students.

Vogaris reads the document.

GREEK LIT. TEACHER: Who is the national poet?

PRINCIPAL: This gentleman.

The gentleman half-rises from his chair.

GENTLEMAN: It is an honor for me . . .

Vogaris looks him over carefully. At first the gentleman is flattered, then he begins to feel uncomfortable.

GREEK LIT. TEACHER: (*to the principal*) And then sell his poems to the boys.

The principal makes a gesture of agreement. The gentleman interrupts him in an effort to explain.

GENTLEMAN: It is not exactly about selling them. Just a token contribution.

He bends over and takes from the carton left on the chair next to him a poorly printed 4-page handout.

GENTLEMAN: Just to cover expenses. Paper, printing, and travel expenses . . .

Vogaris keeps staring at him, serious, without speaking. The gentleman feels even more uncomfortable. He tries desperately to say something intelligent.

GENTLEMAN: Not even a day's wages. But you know this better than anyone . . . poetry cannot be paid for.

He stops. He smiles, embarrassed. Vogaris turns toward the principal.

GREEK LIT. TEACHER: But this is not for someone in my position to decide. You are the one to decide.

The principal smiles with imperceptible irony.

PRINCIPAL: I have already decided. The official document, as you can see, recommends a short introduction.

Vogaris says nothing.

PRINCIPAL: Of course, I cannot insist that you do this.

GENTLEMAN: I would consider it an exceptional honor.

PRINCIPAL: Perhaps with a touch of humor to it.

GREEK LIT. TEACHER: I'm afraid I am completely unprepared for something like this, Mr. Principal, Sir.

In the embarrassment that follows the bell is heard outside signaling the commencement of classes.

50.

The school yard filled with boys. Some at the exit gate, around the stand with the nuts and candies. The bell stops ringing. The classes are assembled. The last straggling children run to their seats. The two gym teachers between the lines. Many of the other teachers under the metal awning.

From the door of his office the principal emerges. He is followed by the poet. Behind them, the woman in charge carrying the carton. They are like a small parade. The principal steps up on the appropriate pedestal. Next to him the poet. The woman in charge places the carton at the latter's feet. The principal is serious and remote.

PRINCIPAL: Our national poet, Mister . . .

He stops and, having again forgotten his name, he turns toward the poet.

GENTLEMAN: Trikorfiotis.

PRINCIPAL: The national poet, Mr. Trikorfiotis will recite his poems to you. They are patriotic in content, and afterward you have the option to purchase copies. I repeat, this is optional. Mr. Trikorfiotis's poems are in this carton.

He points to them and, still serious and remote, he goes and stands with the other teachers. The poet bows gracefully, and with equal grace applauds the departing principal and readies himself to begin reciting. He clears his throat, and so on and so forth. His poems are rhymed along the lines of "land" and "withstand" or "blood" and "flood." His recital is accompanied by the corresponding gestures. In the end, however, he somehow "wins over" the audience. The boys, carried along by the teachers who can barely hide their laughter, begin to enjoy all this too. Kosmas seizes the opportunity, motions to Nikos, and they move discreetly to the back and sneak out.

51.

They go outside. Kosmas buys a paper cone-full of roasted pumpkin seeds from the stand, while behind them the voice of the poet and the laughter of the children can be heard. They detour round the courthouse and come out at the main square. It is a cold, clear day. A biting cold sun. The square is deserted at that moment. In front of the Mainalon Hotel a number of bare tables are spread out, and at the bottom of the square a trash collector slowly pushes his carriage. Kosmas and Nikos cross the square and head for the large park. Suddenly behind them the trot of a horse can be heard. It is accompanied by the soft rhythmic sound of the bells on its collar. They turn toward the sound. A one-horse buggy is passing in front of the courthouse. Its hood drawn back, a beautiful woman seated inside. She seems cheerful, she glances breezily around her, and stares at them insistently, as though sending them a provocative smile.

Kosmas whispers.

KOSMAS: The "Africana."

They stand there until the buggy disappears.

KOSMAS: Do you know something?

They have turned around and continue on their way.

KOSMAS: Gentlemen come all the way from Argos by taxi just because of her.

Nikos stops short and looks at him suspiciously.

NIKOS: How do you know this?

KOSMAS: I heard it from Nikolas. Koularmanis.

Nikos becomes indifferent again.

KOSMAS: I suggest as soon as exams are over we pay her a visit.

NIKOS: (*sarcastically*) To do what?

KOSMAS: What everyone does at such establishments.

They have now reached the entrance to the park.

KOSMAS: Mihalis insists that we three can spend a night with her. In his room. He'll let us use it. His cousin, who is a client of hers, says he can arrange it. And he says she's really worth it. I heard him describe her, describe the positions she takes. She likes to get on her knees, by herself. Know what I mean, when she wants to, she doesn't just do it professionally, she enjoys it.

Nikos grows resentful.

NIKOS: Can't you stop all this talk?

KOSMAS: Stop it, my friend, of course. But I need to know how I can organize our trio. If you'll be part of it or if I should look for someone else.

NIKOS: (*brusquely*) Look for someone else.

Kosmas stops talking and stares at him. Nikos, avoiding his stare, has turned toward the back of the park. A pile of wet dead leaves is slowly burning there. The heavy odorless smoke unhurriedly twists itself into strange obscene shapes.

KOSMAS: We're still friends, right?

Nikos takes out two cigarettes.

NIKOS: Want one?
KOSMAS: No.

Nikos lights up, takes a first puff, and refocuses his gaze on the smoke.

KOSMAS: And I'll save your place. The trio can't be changed.

Nikos can no longer stand up to Kosmas's persistent pressure. A short nervous laugh escapes him inadvertently. He turns toward Kosmas now twice as angry, but he stays put. An old dump truck has come into the square and is moving toward the center. There it makes a U-turn, stops, and begins slowly raising its carriage as a sergeant with cartridge pouches and a tommy-gun steps out of the front of the truck. Intrigued, Kosmas also turns to look at it. From the raised carriage bodies have already begun to fall.

52.

They are the first to reach the scene. After a while the circle of spectators increases. In the middle a small pyramid of dead men has formed. The sole woman among them lies on her stomach capping the pyramid. Her skirt has been pulled up to her buttocks and on the outside of her left thigh a bayonet wound is visible. In spite of the shudder of death on her skin, intensified by the winter sun, Kosmas is wildly aroused. The first comments can already be heard around them.

One version: The Special Mountain Combat Units wiped out this small section in a nighttime raid.

Another version: They had taken them captive. Someone tried to escape and they executed them all.

Kosmas turns and looks at Nikos. His eyes too are transfixed by the nudity of the dead woman. Maddened by the clarity of the air, a flock of crows circles round over the trees in the park.

θεί τον πα-
κενηντόρης,
ς μεγάλο σί-

Μας άλλαζον

DAY ELEVEN

53.

Kosmas in his room. On his table an open history book. He tries to study, but without enthusiasm. Suddenly he hears a whistle from outside — a password of sorts. He strains to hear it. The whistling is repeated. He opens the door and steps outside. Past the cement walkway, outside the small garden gate, stands Nikos. Kosmas motions to him.

KOSMAS: Come on in.

Nikos opens the small door and steps inside.

NIKOS: Are you studying?
KOSMAS: I'm trying to. What about you?
NIKOS: I gave up. I can't pull myself together.

They go into the room.

KOSMAS: Which exam do we have tomorrow?

Nikos doesn't answer. He looks at the book on the table.

NIKOS: How much have you done?

He takes the book in his hands. He glances at the page it is opened at and comes up with a question.

NIKOS: When was the Kioutsouk-Kaïnartzi treaty signed?

KOSMAS: On July 21. In the year 1774, otherwise known as the treaty of eternal peace.

NIKOS: Bull's eye. Good for you.

KOSMAS: I just saw it a minute ago. What do you mean bull's eye?

Nikos puts the book back on the table.

NIKOS: I'll at least let you study.

KOSMAS: Bullshit, me study?

He closes the book and tosses it to the other side of the room.

KOSMAS: Where are you going?

NIKOS: (*shrugging his shoulders*) Anywhere at all.

54.

The railroad station deserted. Cloudy skies. Nikos and Kosmas walk onto the platform. Killing time. They look at the board with the train schedules, then at the large clock hanging under the metal awning. Five minutes past four. An employee in a uniform and cap comes out from one door and goes into another. Kosmas walks over and peers inside. The telegraph machine is running by itself and the tape flaps and jerks every so often. He turns back toward Nikos. He is standing further back, at the edge of the tracks, and is looking in the exact opposite direction. Kosmas goes over to him without speaking. Some way off, in the distance, a low fenced-in house. Nikos looks at Kosmas.

55.

At the corner of the house, although it is still daytime, a small bare light bulb is burning. Nikos and Kosmas stand outside hesitant. They do not even dare to admit that they haven't the courage to go inside. In the end they are saved from their dilemma by a second door inside the surrounding stone fence. It opens suddenly and as it does the national poet appears, with his ascot and his boots. Kosmas and Nikos spring nimbly to their left, turn at the stone wall and end up at its back corner. They press themselves against the wall. In front of them is a pothole with greenish water. Hundreds of used prophylactics are rotting there. Waiting for the poet to move away Nikos takes out two cigarettes. He offers one to Kosmas. He takes it. Nikos lights it for him, then lights his own. Kosmas inhales the smoke carefully, he keeps it for a minute in his mouth and then lets it out in small swirls, with his gaze fixed on the water in the pothole, which has begun to ripple. It is raining lightly. He takes a second puff and, continuing to stare at the surface of the greenish water, he begins to recite.

KOSMAS: You enter through the sitting room. You choose a woman. You signal to her with your eyes. Or you tell her "Let's go." She shows you the door to her room. You go inside. Alone. You take off your pants. Then everything else. And she comes in.

• • •

A NOTE ON THE TRANSLATION

The text of Thanassis Valtinos's *New Moon: Day One* alternates simple descriptive passages in his signature concise, elliptical prose, whose debt to cinema and theater writing is worth noting, with snippets of dialog that are realistic-sounding and colloquial in tone and equally influenced, certainly in part, by cinema and theater conversational effects.

This translation aims to bring across and underscore the contrast between the artful lyricism and musicality of the descriptive passages and the contemporary thrust of the dialog, be it the vernacular of the high school students themselves or the often more formal style of their Greek literature teacher and their high school principal — a multifaceted collage in different styles, to put it mildly, and a classic Valtinos technique culminating in his 1989 documentary novel *Data from the Decade of the Sixties.*[14]

For the central conversational tones of the dialog between the adolescent protagonists and their friends in *New Moon: Day One,* a middle-of-the-road strategy of translation was used, one which follows the Greek rendering and downplays the 1946–1947 adolescent Greek slang because, very much like J. D. Salinger's slang, as for example in *The Catcher in the Rye* of the same time period, it too sounds quite dated today. Using very contemporary adolescent slang, on the other hand, would underplay the fact that the story takes place in Greece during the Civil War and would have detracted from the historical feel of the original. Simply put, the youths' conversations in *New Moon: Day One* are meant to come across, as in the original, as neither dated nor overly contemporary.

14. Original Greek title: *Stoicheia yia ti dekaetia tou '60*. English translation, *Data from the Decade of the Sixties*, tr. Jane Assimakopoulos, Stavros Deligiorgis, Northwestern University Press, Evanston, Illinois, 2000.

The descriptive passages, on the other hand, often focusing on or preceding intervals of silence, are in stark contrast to the loquaciousness in the dialogs. They are, like Valtinos's prose in general, and in spite of their economical compactness (similar in brevity to stage directions), more lyrical in tone, and possess an innate musicality typical of Valtinos's discursive writing in general.

The lyrical overtones in these passages are created, in part, by the artful juxtaposition and alternation of simple descriptive sentences (i.e., "the sun is descending in the west") with truncated, often verbless, phrases, such as "Kosmas and Nikos on their bicycles. Moving at a steady pace." Not only have these alternations been kept in this translation, but also, to keep them from becoming monotonous, they have been reinforced by taking advantage of the English-language duality between the simple indicative present and its continuous counterpart (a duality that does not exist in Greek) and alternating these two present tenses, as in "Some students are taking notes. Others simply watch."

Aside from the obvious prerequisite of translation, that is, accuracy on the level of specific words and their meaning, the style and "voice" of the original also needed to be addressed. Greek idiomatic expressions on occasion called for interpretive interventions in the text, as when the narrator describes a promotional placard for a Rita Hayworth movie in the original Greek as containing photographs of actresses in "nude" poses. "Nude," to the Greek readers in the rather "Victorian" times of Greece in the 1940s, implied little more than "not fully clothed," i.e., low necklines and provocatively hiked-up skirts in movies and their promotional advertising. Viewed in this particular cultural setting the flavor and the actual intended meaning of the description of the placard demanded an equivalent, interpretive rendering as in "photographs . . . with flesh exposed" rather than a literal translation of the Greek.

The main goal of this translation, in spite of the pronounced modulations across numerous sections of the Greek original, has been, above all, to create a texture as precise and as convincingly literary in English as it is in the Greek.

New Moon: Day One is an outstanding cultural artifact that is, through and through, so quintessentially Greek (and not merely by virtue of the language it is written in) that the only way to do justice to its timeless importance was to create and recreate its artfulness so that, in all its different ways, it would also be perceived as quintessentially English. It is hoped that the present translation has achieved this.

BIOGRAPHIES

Thanassis Valtinos was born in 1932 in Kastri, Kynourias, in the Peloponnese. He has written novels, novellas, short stories, and film scripts and translated ancient Greek tragedies for the theater. His work has been translated into many languages and has earned him numerous awards, including Best Screenplay (Cannes Film Festival 1984), the Greek State Prize for Best Novel (1990), the International Cavafy Prize (2002), the Petros Haris Prize, conferred by the Academy of Athens for Lifetime Achievement (2002), the Gold Cross of Honor of the President of the Greek Democracy (2003), and the Greek State Prize for Lifetime Achievement (2012). In 2008 he was elected a member of the Greek Academy and served as its president in 2016.

Jane Assimakopoulos is an American writer and translator living in Ioannina, Greece. Her translations from the Greek and French include novels by award-winning writers as well as poems and stories in literary journals and anthologies in the U.S. and in England. Between 1999 and 2018 she was employed by a Greek publisher as translation editor in charge of a series of books by Philip Roth.

Stavros Deligiorgis is a University of Iowa professor emeritus. He was educated in Bucharest, Romania, in the U.S., and Athens, Greece, where he lives and works at present. He taught courses in English and American literature and comparative literature (classics; Old and Middle English) at the University of Iowa and as a visiting professor at several U.S. and European universities. He has authored studies in literary theory as well as collections of translations from the Greek, Romanian, Italian, and Old Provençal languages. In 2021 he was awarded an honorary doctorate in Philosophy by the National and Capodistrian University of Athens.

Other works of Thanassis Valtinos translated by Jane Assimakopoulos and Stavros Deligiorgis:

Deep Blue Almost Black: Selected Fiction
Evanston, Illinois: Northwestern University Press, Hydra Books, 1997.

Data from the Decade of the Sixties
Evanston, Illinois: Northwestern University Press, Hydra Books, 2000.

Orthokostá: A Novel
Foreword by Stathis N. Kalyvas, New Haven and London: Yale University Press, The Margellos World Republic of Letters, 2016.

Thanassis Valtinos: Early Works
Chapel Hill, North Carolina: Laertes Press, 2021.